# The Passengers on the Hankyu Line

Berkley Titles by Hiro Arikawa

*The Travelling Cat Chronicles*
(Translated by Philip Gabriel)

*The Goodbye Cat*
(Translated by Philip Gabriel)

*The Passengers on the Hankyu Line*
(Translated by Allison Markin Powell)

# The Passengers on the Hankyu Line

## HIRO ARIKAWA

Translated from Japanese
by Allison Markin Powell

BERKLEY ∫ NEW YORK

BERKLEY
An imprint of Penguin Random House LLC
1745 Broadway, New York, NY 10019
penguinrandomhouse.com

*Hankyu Densha* by Hiro Arikawa copyright © 2008 by Hiro Arikawa
Translation copyright © 2025 by Allison Markin Powell
First published in the United Kingdom, in 2025, by Doubleday, an imprint of Transworld.
Transworld is part of the Penguin Random House group of companies.
Penguin Random House values and supports copyright. Copyright fuels creativity,
encourages diverse voices, promotes free speech, and creates a vibrant culture.
Thank you for buying an authorized edition of this book and for complying with copyright
laws by not reproducing, scanning, or distributing any part of it in any form without permission.
You are supporting writers and allowing Penguin Random House to continue to publish
books for every reader. Please note that no part of this book may be used or reproduced
in any manner for the purpose of training artificial intelligence technologies or systems.

BERKLEY and the BERKLEY & B colophon are registered trademarks of
Penguin Random House LLC.

Text illustrations © Xuan Loc Xuan
Map page design by Anthony Maddock/TW
Title and part page art: Mountains © Ichpochmak/Shutterstock

Original Japanese edition published by Gentosha Inc., Tokyo.
English language translation rights arranged with Gentosha Inc. through
The English Agency (Japan) Ltd. and New River Literary Ltd.

Library of Congress Cataloging-in-Publication Data

Names: Arikawa, Hiro, 1972– author. | Powell, Allison Markin, translator.
Title: The passengers on the Hankyu line / Hiro Arikawa;
translated from Japanese by Allison Markin Powell.
Other titles: Hankyū densha. English
Description: New York: Berkley, 2025.
Identifiers: LCCN 2024059617 (print) | LCCN 2024409202 (ebook) |
ISBN 9798217187188 (hardcover) | ISBN 9798217187195 (ebook)
Subjects: LCGFT: Novels.
Classification: LCC PL867.5.R54 H3613 2025 (print) |
LCC PL867.5.R54 (ebook) | DDC [Fic]—dc23
LC record available at https://lccn.loc.gov/2024059617
LC ebook record available at https://lccn.loc.gov/2024409202

Printed in the United States of America
1st Printing

The authorized representative in the EU for product safety and compliance is
Penguin Random House Ireland, Morrison Chambers, 32 Nassau Street,
Dublin D02 YH68, Ireland, https://eu-contact.penguin.ie.

All manner of people from every walk of life—
solo passengers, friends, couples, families, work
colleagues—traverse the concourse at a brisk pace.

But as they cross paths, the contents of each
traveler's heart are a mystery known only to
themselves.

HIRO ARIKAWA

CONTENTS

Map *xi*
Author's Note *xiii*
Dramatis Personae *xv*

## *Bound for Nishinomiya-Kitaguchi*

Takarazuka Station *3*
Takarazuka-Minamiguchi Station *15*
Sakasegawa Station *31*
Obayashi Station *47*
Nigawa Station *61*
Koto'en Station *73*
Mondo Yakujin Station *87*
Nishinomiya-Kitaguchi Station *101*

AND THEN BACK AGAIN

## *Bound for Takarazuka*

Nishinomiya-Kitaguchi Station *121*
Mondo Yakujin Station *139*
Koto'en Station *153*

## Contents

Nigawa Station  *167*
Obayashi Station  *183*
Sakasegawa Station  *199*
Takarazuka-Minamiguchi Station  *213*

AND THEN

Takarazuka Station  *229*

| Northbound | Southbound |
|---|---|
| TAKARAZUKA | NISHINOMIYA-KITAGUCHI |
| TAKARAZUKA-MINAMIGUCHI | MONDO YAKUJIN |
| SAKASEGAWA | KOTO'EN |
| OBAYASHI | NIGAWA |
| NIGAWA | OBAYASHI |
| KOTO'EN | SAKASEGAWA |
| MONDO YAKUJIN | TAKARAZUKA-MINAMIGUCHI |
| NISHINOMIYA-KITAGUCHI | TAKARAZUKA |

# AUTHOR'S NOTE

At Takarazuka Station on the Hankyu Railway Line, the Takarazuka Line bound for Umeda in Osaka and the Imazu Line that connects with the Kobe Line at Nishinomiya-Kitaguchi Station converge in a Y shape, which in railway terminology is called a wye. Here you can also transfer to the JR Takarazuka Line, which makes Takarazuka Station a fairly large junction of three railway lines for this relatively regional mountainous area in western Japan.

Hankyu is a large private commuter railway line that operates in Kansai—as the area surrounding Kyoto, Osaka and Kobe is known—and its signature maroon train cars with their distinctive retro interiors are very popular among railway buffs, as well as with young women.

This story takes place along the Imazu Line, perhaps one of the lesser known among Hankyu's various train lines.

## DRAMATIS PERSONAE
(in order of appearance)

MASASHI, an office worker
YUKI, an office worker
SHOKO, an office worker
TOKIÉ, grandmother of Ami
AMI, granddaughter of Tokié
MISA, a student at a women's college
KATSUYA, a college student and Misa's boyfriend
ETSUKO ("ET-CHAN"), a high school student
KEI'ICHI, a university student
MIHO ("GON-CHAN"), a university student
YASUÉ ("ITOH-SAN"), a housewife and mother

# The Passengers on the Hankyu Line

*Bound for
Nishinomiya-Kitaguchi*

# Takarazuka Station

L one passengers, for the most part, show no expression, often appearing to be in their own world. They stare at the landscape whizzing by or at the ads hanging inside the car, or if their eyes do happen to wander around the carriage, they avoid meeting anyone else's gaze. Otherwise, they pass their time on the train in the usual ways—reading a book or listening to music or staring at their mobile phone.

That is why
a person alone
without any kind of distraction
looking animated
is very conspicuous.

On this particular day, the young woman who got on at Takarazuka Station and sat next to Masashi looked familiar—or at least *he* recognized *her*.

If you were to transfer from the Imazu Line to the Takarazuka Line and ride one stop to Kiyoshikojin Station, you would find Takarazuka Central Library.

In the five years since Masashi had started working in an

office, he would visit this library every two weeks or so. He did like to read and sometimes he had research to do for work, but on days off when he didn't have plans and since he didn't have a girlfriend, there wasn't really much else to do.

So Masashi was enough of a regular that he soon got to know the library staff, as well as a couple of the other patrons. Enough to recognize when that pesky old guy was giving the librarian a hard time again, and so on.

He remembered the young woman with the long neat hair because he had once lost out to her in the scramble for a book.

It was a buzzy new book that happened to be back on the shelf.

This was only about a month after it had been released, so it seemed pretty lucky. In an instant, Masashi had reached for the book, but just as he did so, another hand suddenly snatched it away.

With a frown, he looked around to see who had nabbed the book—an attractive young woman—and so any impulse to complain vanished. Men are weak.

The young woman seemed unaware she had just snatched the book—she had not even seen him. Masashi watched, following after her for a few minutes, but gave up once it was obvious she was not letting it go.

At the time, the young woman had been carrying a canvas tote bag featuring a certain internationally recognizable mouse. He had found it a bit childish for someone her age—but then again, maybe it was the sturdiest bag she owned, or one that she didn't care if it got ruined. When lugging around the maximum number of books you could borrow from the library, a flimsier or more tasteful bag would soon get damaged.

Which meant that she must come here pretty often.

His assumption was right on the money—since he came to the library fairly often himself, he started noticing her there more frequently. He'd spot her by her bag, emblazoned with the image of that mouse, its mouth wide open in a smile. She really was Masashi's type, though, and although hard to admit, he quickly got used to seeking out the rodent.

Having lost out to her the one time, Masashi considered her a rival, so whenever he saw her around, he'd scour the library's shelves preemptively for any special books that might be available.

He soon realized they shared similar tastes.

She had a knack for discovering interesting books, and as he threw a grudging glance at her selection, he'd consider borrowing them himself after she returned them. But he never made a note of the titles and soon forgot what any of them were.

He only ever bumped into her at the library—until now, they had never found themselves on the same train home.

At Kiyoshikojin Station, she had gotten on the train headed for Takarazuka Station, boarding the same car as Masashi, her tote with the smiling happy-go-lucky mouse bulging as always. Not that Masashi was one to talk—his leather backpack was filled to bursting.

But only Masashi seemed to have noticed.

At Takarazuka Station, where the train terminates, there are three options: leave the station, or transfer to the JR line or to the other train line for Nishinomiya-Kitaguchi, known as Nishi-Kita.

*No way, she can't be heading for Nishi-Kita . . .* he thought, but as their train pulled into the station, her gaze was locked on the opposite platform.

And sure enough, as soon as they arrived, she scurried over toward the train that was sitting at the platform across the way. On weekends, due to the popularity of the Hanshin Racecourse at Nigawa, all four tracks would often be occupied, with trains for Umeda and Takarazuka, and Nishinomiya-Kitaguchi and Takarazuka, respectively, sitting opposite each other. So the transfer time was minor.

*The same track, even?* His eyes followed her with vague annoyance, and he decided to travel in a different carriage.

It was pretty crowded, but the books he had taken out from the library were heavy, so Masashi managed to score one of the empty seats.

Just then, the interior door connecting the cars opened. And who should appear but the young woman herself. *Not many empty seats*, she seemed to be thinking, swaying as she made her way down the carriage.

There were still a few empty seats. Without hesitating, she took the closest one, next to Masashi.

Such a strange series of chance encounters, overlapping like Jenga pieces, even if Masashi seemed to be the only one aware they were two players in a game.

Masashi hastily pulled one of the books he'd borrowed from his backpack.

As he began flipping through the pages, the young woman beside him made an odd motion. The famous mouse tote bag, heavy with books, still on her lap, she had swiveled her body around to see fully out of the window. She was now turned toward Masashi, so he had a full view of her face without even trying.

She was smiling and looking down at the scene below the elevated railway tracks.

*What is it?* Masashi peered down below too. The train was going over the iron bridge that spans the Mukogawa River.

"Huh?"

The sound came out involuntarily. On a sandbank in the river, just before they reached the other side of the iron bridge, not small by any means but rather taking up almost the entire area above the waterline, someone had written a character:

生

Or, not written so much as assembled—stones were piled up to form a three-dimensional shape of the kanji for "life."

It had just the right balance and stature to catch the eye as an impressive objet d'art.

"Amazing, isn't it?"

The character 生 was so huge that it could be clearly made out, even from a distance and at an angle. But it wasn't until the train had gotten to the other side of the bridge that he realized she was speaking to him.

While he was processing this fact, the young woman carried on speaking.

"I first saw it about a month ago. It's amazing, right?"

*What's amazing is that you even spotted it*, he murmured. That she would focus her attention on a sandbank where no one would think to look and then notice some graffiti (?) there was kind of ridiculous—and yet remarkable.

"Why do you think it's amazing?" she asked.

He paused for a moment. "... I guess it's the shape. The lines are so bold and its height so even, as if someone used heavy machinery. Must've taken a lot of guts, just for a prank."

"I think the choice of character is pretty amazing," she said. "That kanji has straight lines, which makes it easy to construct. And for a single character on its own, it's impactful, right? The first time I saw it, it made me thirsty for a beer."

"Ahh, so you read it as *'nama,'* as in 'draft beer'? I thought it was *'sei,'* like 'life or death.'"

"Oh, that works too. I'm sure they meant for it to be taken both ways."

"If you really want to know, maybe you could ask about it at the town hall? It might be a river works project."

"Oh, I won't do that." She pursed her lips and shook her head. "I might find out that it's something practical—maybe it's groundwork for some construction or maybe it's just some graffiti that's about to be removed—that would ruin it. I kind of hope that it's graffiti. I mean, if it's a prank, it's rare to see one so sophisticated and so memorable. I'm OK with not knowing what the meaning of it is, and I hope it stays there forever."

*She has a point*, he thought to himself.

The graffiti had been created for its own sake; its impact would never be known. It cheered him a bit to imagine that whoever had come up with it must be living in the same city as him.

"It'd be cool if it were supposed to be *'nama'* ... " Masashi muttered, and she tilted her head inquiringly. "But if it's read as '*sei*,' then you can't help thinking it's about 'how to live' or 'life or death,' right? So then, as a fun piece of graffiti, there must be some kind of message . . . like a prayer or something."

Her expression shifted before his eyes, from amusement to disappointment.

*Yikes*, he thought. *I screwed up!*

He hadn't intended to spoil her excitement. The only reason he had even noticed her was because he had lost out to her in the scramble for a book, but he hadn't meant to seek out any kind of retaliation.

"I, uh . . . see what you mean. I guess it might not be just a fun prank. It could be for someone who's not well, and their family made that character as a sort of prayer or something."

"Th-that's not what I meant at all!" Masashi interrupted. "If you think about it, the landscape along this railway line is jam-packed with temples and shrines and monks."

Along the Takarazuka Line is an old pilgrimage route known as the Junrei Kaido—starting with the station after Takarazuka, the next three stations are each home to various Buddhist temples and Shinto shrines: Kiyoshikojin Station, the one closest to Takarazuka Central Library, is named after Kiyoshikojin Seichoji Temple; the next station, Mefu Jinja, is named for the albeit minor though deeply rooted with local constituents Mefu Shrine; and the station after that is home to one of the most popular temples in the region, Nakayama-dera.

Finally, on the Imazu Line, the station before Nishi-Kita is named for the thriving temple Mondo Yakujin Tokoji, where people go to pray.

"Rather than creating such an odd prayer, surely paying a

visit to a nearby temple or shrine would be faster! Especially when you can have your pick of so many around here!"

"Do you really think so?"

"Trying to guess what it could possibly mean, there are a mess of possibilities. Like, it could be just a playful joke, or a prayer like I said—but then it could also be a curse."

"A *curse*?! What gives you that idea?!"

"Well, if you read it as the word for 'life,' the idea of writing something like that on a sandbank in the river, where the water is going to wash it away, doesn't it have a sense of the occult or some creepy horror thing? I can easily see how a student who's into that kind of stuff could have done it."

"Wow, I never thought of that!" She pouted. "It's been a month since I first noticed it. And already, my imagination pales in comparison to yours, and you've only just seen it."

"Hmm . . . you're being surprisingly competitive."

"I mean, I just took it to be a lark, and nothing more."

Even though she beat him in the book scramble, she seemed pretty nice. She saw a cryptic character written on a sandbank and immediately accepted the most lighthearted and harmless explanation—it even made her crave a beer.

"NEXT STOP, SAKASEGAWA," came the announcement on the train. Apparently they had passed the preceding station, Takarazuka-Minamiguchi, without noticing.

"Oh, this is my stop," she said with a slight nod of her head.

"Sakasegawa, huh? I wanted to live in that area myself. When I moved here, that was the first place I looked, but I couldn't find anything there."

He'd made this random comment, apropos of nothing, perhaps as a way to keep their conversation going.

"Really? I wonder why not? I found a place near the station right away."

"Might be that Sakasegawa is close to the Takarazuka theater? I guess a lot of fans want to live there too. I had a real estate broker looking for me, but they said the only places available were just for women or were family oriented."

"Is that so? The town hall is there too, so I guess it's a pretty convenient location."

The train began to slow, and she stood up from her seat.

*OK then.* She waved a hand, and he waved back.

"I'm gonna get myself a beer on the way home today. In support of your theory. It's the most fun version, right?" he said.

She had been heading for the doors, but she turned back toward him.

"The next time we meet, we should have a drink. I prefer beer in a glass mug rather than in a can."

*Hey, what'd she mean by "the next time"?* Masashi thought, bewildered. They hadn't even exchanged contact information. As far as she was concerned, he was just a stranger she'd struck up a conversation with about some charming graffiti.

"The central library. You go there a lot, don't you? So then, next time we meet."

He was speechless—at that moment the train stopped and the doors opened, and with a spring in her step, she alighted from the train.

She headed for the staircase rather than use the escalator,

that bag on her shoulder with the mouse, its mouth open in a gaping smile.

As Masashi watched it swaying awkwardly, his hands reflexively popped up to cover his mouth.

*So she* had *noticed him after all*, he thought, his cheeks uncharacteristically flushed.

*The next time we meet.*

Today's Saturday. Nothing special lined up, just a regular old boring afternoon.

He'd thought that he was the only one aware of their chance encounters.

When? And where?

He had the sudden urge to run off the train to find out why she had been the one to home in on him.

If she wanted to drink beer out of a glass, then why not today?!

Masashi got up from his seat and leaped onto the platform.

The mouse with the full-faced smile was only halfway up the long staircase. Masashi started up the stairs, taking them two at a time to catch up with her.

# Takarazuka-Minamiguchi Station

Takarazuka-Minamiguchi is a run-down train station in dire need of renovation.

Whereas its neighboring stations on either side—Takarazuka and Sakasegawa, and for that matter all the other stations along the same line—have a bustling and lively vibe, Takarazuka-Minamiguchi seems to be the only one left behind in that wave of development.

There is a two-story shopping mall that, up until some years ago, had still been sparsely populated by ramshackle shops, but after the few that were left had been evicted in advance of these renovation plans, no progress had been made.

The only attraction there is perhaps the Takarazuka Hotel. It's said that for fans of the Takarazuka Revue, an all-female musical theater troupe, there's an excellent chance of spotting one of their stars at this prestigious hotel.

As Shoko boarded the Nishi-Kita–bound train after it had slid into the platform, the clicking of her heels seemed to resonate intimidatingly. The train car wasn't crowded but almost all the seats were taken, so, in her white dress, Shoko was hovering near the door. If she squeezed into one of the available seats, she would wrinkle the skirt of her dress, which had cost her a pretty yen.

Carelessly, she allowed a bag engraved with the emblem of the Takarazuka Hotel—no doubt containing a wedding favor—to drop by her feet. What did she care how fragile whatever was inside might be? After all, if she'd been happy to receive the favor, she wouldn't have attended the occasion dressed all in white.

She would never forget the look on the bride's face when she laid eyes on Shoko wearing what might as well have been a wedding dress. Yes, she would tuck that memory away in a corner of her heart.

White was the bride's color—guests knew better than to wear it. That was the most basic rule of the dress code for weddings. Shoko's hair was even done up and adorned with white accessories. From the moment she arrived at the reception and signed the registry book, the other guests had been giving her looks and rolling their eyes.

She had to laugh, no?

Recalling the looks on their faces, the corners of Shoko's mouth turned up in a smile.

*I can't believe you'd do such a thing to me.*

They had worked at the same company for five years. She had started to date the groom six months after they started working together. The company had sanctioned their relationship, so they were publicly a couple, and once they were into their third year, everyone at the office had thought that it wouldn't be long before Shoko and the groom got married.

The bride joined the company at the same time and had also been a friend. Past tense, of course—though there's no way for Shoko to know just when that became so.

In contrast to Shoko, with her striking features and brisk

manner, the bride was a rather ordinary girl who seemed to have turned into an equally ordinary office worker.

They had been on the same team during training, and the bride had become attached to Shoko, who was anything but shy and had made various friends and connections at the office. The bride was the quiet type who always seemed to stealthily insert herself into Shoko's circle.

*Why are you friends with the likes of her? You're nothing like each other.* Someone had once asked Shoko this when the bride wasn't around.

For the life of her, Shoko didn't recall why or how. During training, she had felt like the quiet-type bride was dependent on her, and then before Shoko knew it, she was already cosied up with her. Shoko didn't find anything to dislike about being around her, and at work the bride neither sprinted ahead nor dragged anyone down, so they had remained friendly. Shoko hadn't paid much attention to her, though the bride continued to stick close to Shoko.

Then, when Shoko started dating the groom, the bride must have heard about it through the grapevine, because she had asked Shoko, "You're seeing X now?"

"Yes, well," Shoko had replied, not wanting to publicize matters of her personal life.

"Why didn't you tell me?" the bride had asked in a gently chiding tone.

"We aren't friends." Pressed to explain herself, for just a brief moment Shoko had thought, *Ugh, she's so annoying.*

In retrospect, that's when Shoko ought to have distanced herself. But since they worked together and she did not want to spark any conflict, she had opted for prudence.

*If only I had cut ties back then* . . . Yet it was a waste of time to contemplate what was irreversible, so she wouldn't bother thinking about it.

"A *curse?!*"

She heard a woman in a nearby seat exclaim. Her tone of voice as well as the incongruity of the word made Shoko glance quickly over at the couple sitting there. They were both dressed casually, but Shoko took them to be career types. What stood out about them was that they were both carrying bags that were full to bursting.

"What gives you that idea?!"

"Well, if you read it as the word for 'life' . . . "

The young woman was consumed with curiosity, while the young man appeared to be more aware of his surroundings, so he had lowered his voice in an effort to mollify her. It worked quite well. Shoko could no longer hear their conversation from where she was standing.

*A curse?*

Shoko let out an involuntary snort.

Perhaps she too had engaged in a skirmish of sorts—using the white dress she was wearing to cast the spell of her own curse.

∽

In the fifth year of their relationship, the subject of marriage increasingly came up in conversation. They both seemed to suffer from premarital anxiety—they argued more frequently and were often at odds with each other.

It won't last, just hold out until the wedding, her married friend had advised, and Shoko had believed her.

However, that advice had been based upon the assumption that there wasn't someone waiting in the wings, someone who would prey upon that premarital anxiety and use it to her own advantage.

He wasn't a very good liar, and Shoko's instincts told her that he was having an affair. Though since they were both going through a period of uncertainty, she had thought she'd be able to forgive him—whether he chose to confess or not.

But then she had been gobsmacked to see that very same quiet type sitting beside him at the restaurant where she had been summoned.

*Her?*

"We should break up."

Why were those words being directed at her? It made absolutely no sense.

"You owe me an explanation."

Shoko's response was not meant for him but instead for the quiet type, who drew herself close to him, looking frightened.

In silence, he produced a pink notebook. It was a pregnancy planner—and it had the quiet type's name on it.

Shoko was utterly speechless.

". . . You mean to say that you cheated on me while we were planning our wedding—and that you did it in the raw?!"

Shoko blurted out this vulgar phrase—there was no time to choose her words carefully—and the quiet type spoke up in tears.

"I'm sorry, it's my fault. I was the one who said he didn't

need to use anything. I told him that if I got pregnant, I'd have an abortion so it wouldn't cause any trouble."

And this fool, he'd believed what she said.

In that moment, it dawned on her, calmly and clearly. That the man she'd been with all this time, the man she'd thought she was going to marry, was this much of a witless chump.

"So you just leaped at the offer, did you? Because she told you she'd get rid of it if she got pregnant. Do you have any idea how disgusting that makes you?"

*Ugh, it was so awful.* She was aware that the people around them were eavesdropping. How humiliating to be associated with such a sordid pair.

"And what else've you got to say for yourself?"

Shoko gestured toward the quiet type with her chin. It was obvious to Shoko that she was fake crying, but she managed to respond.

"I've had feelings for X ever since I started working at the company . . . so when I realized that I was pregnant, it turned out . . . I said that I would raise the child on my own, he didn't even have to acknowledge us."

*What a load of crap. You must have delivered that line to him, anticipating that he'd be taken in by it.*

Though she didn't know whether to be glad or sad that he could be taken in like that.

"You're strong, Shoko—I know you have what it takes to be on your own," he said.

*Don't feed me the lyrics to some tawdry pop song! If I can make it on my own, what have I been doing with you for the past five years? Why was I working through all that premarital anxiety with you, then?*

"But now that she's pregnant, and such a quiet type, the kind of woman who would make a good mother and good home . . . I could never be happy, being with you, pretending not to know that she was having my child."

*You're a chump and a fool—do you really think a woman who claims to be my friend while seducing you is really such a quiet and marriageable type?*

"Besides, you're not even crying, are you? Even when this happens to you. Here she is, crying her eyes out, and all you do is get angry and place blame, right? If you were a bit more sympathetic . . ."

"I'd stop there if I were you. You're only making yourself out to be more disgusting, and you'll ruin your chances with her too."

Shoko's warning seemed to land, because he shut up.

Was he really implying that if she were more congenial, he'd have chosen her? That he wouldn't have hesitated to insist that the quiet type have an abortion?

*Enough.*

"I'll allow you to break our engagement on one condition. And if you don't comply with it, I'll sue you for breach of promise."

They'd been together for five years and had been planning their wedding for months. She was well aware of his financial position, that on top of a shotgun wedding he couldn't afford to be hit with a breach of promise and have to pay consolation damages.

The two of them gulped in anticipation of what Shoko's condition would be.

"You must invite me to the wedding."

The quiet type, she was a romantic dreamer. Of course there would be a wedding, in one form or another.

Only now did she look like she was going to cry for real. Which made it all the more obvious that her tears shed previously had been a facade.

When the new couple made the rounds at their company to announce their impending marriage, they were met with uniformly dubious looks from the heads of each department—that was because each of them had already heard about it through Shoko's network. In other words, the backstory of the quiet type sleeping with Shoko's fiancé and getting pregnant, and of him then leaving Shoko, had spread through the office.

All Shoko had to do was maintain a tragic but brave face as she went about her daily tasks—that was enough for the couple's stock to plummet. Shoko had always had a stellar reputation at work, so the bosses' sympathies were with her.

*That slippery woman who glued herself to me like a sharksucker fish only to steal away my soon-to-be husband, and the fool who'd fallen for it hook, line and sinker: don't think the two of you will just live happily ever after.*

Apparently they were making it out to seem as though the wedding would be a modest gathering, only for their inner circle. Shoko heard that one of their superiors had made the blatantly snide remark, "I had been looking forward to attending your wedding, but not so much now that the players have changed."

The wedding day arrived.

It was an intimate ceremony, with only family and the couple's close friends, and Shoko was indeed invited as a "friend of the bride."

From the moment she walked in, Shoko's white dress, whose design could easily be taken for a minimalist wedding dress itself, caused a stir at the reception.

It was a rather tepid event. None of Shoko's acquaintances had been invited. Naturally she and the groom shared mutual friends, but thinking ahead and for the sake of appearances, it seemed he had only invited second-tier acquaintances whom Shoko had never met. It was their misfortune to have to bear the brunt of the celebration.

The bride's guests did not seem to be very close friends of hers either. At work she had disappeared into the crowd by attaching herself to Shoko. Presumably she had done the same during her school years as well.

"That's some dress!"

The compliment was given with a curious look, at which Shoko beamed a smile.

"The bride slept with my man and got herself knocked up, so as the former fiancée, I think I deserve a bit of spitefulness, wouldn't you say?"

Judging by the gleeful squeals of the women at her table, it seemed unlikely that any of them considered the bride a friend.

Never was she gladder to have been gifted with natural beauty than when the bridal couple made their entrance and began to circle around to each table.

Even aided by the talents of a professional makeup artist, the bride was no match for Shoko. And had Shoko been wearing a fancier dress, the disparity would have been more extreme.

The bride's face contorted wildly. She looked back at the

groom with an expression like a Shinto demon, and Shoko knew that she was checking to see where the groom's eyes were at that moment.

And there was no question—

In that instant, the groom was looking at Shoko. At the one who could have been his forever, had he not fallen into the trap laid by the woman he had just married.

"I hope you have a wonderful life together."

Shoko bowed, while the women at her table chimed with a lighthearted "Congratulations!"

When it was time for the photographer to snap the guests with the bridal couple, the bride's voice rang out sharply.

"Not this table! No photos, please!"

*Whaat? Don't be mean! What did we do? You're the one who invited us, so here we are!*

The women at her table played their parts, each of their comments a pinprick stab at the bride. Whether they were uncouth to begin with or whether they were siding with Shoko, either was fine by her.

Shoko herself had come here today knowing full well that the couple would consider her behavior very unladylike.

The MC began to relate an anecdote about why the bride had chosen this hotel—her mother's wedding had taken place here, and she'd wanted her own to be held here too—which may have been meant as a charming story, though it made the earlier scene all the more satisfying for Shoko.

As the lights dimmed for a slideshow, a staff member from the venue approached Shoko from the shadows. "Excuse me," she said, holding out a black shawl. "The bride feels that your outfit is too dramatic, and wonders if you would consider wearing this around your shoulders."

"Very well."

Now was her moment. Shoko stood up quietly.

"Please excuse the interruption. I'm afraid I have to leave; please show me the way out."

Without asking for any further clarification, the staff member immediately guided Shoko to the exit.

Having brought Shoko outside, under the cover of darkness, the staff member offered her a bag with the wedding favor inside. Shoko tried to refuse, but the staff member bowed politely.

"I would be reprimanded for failing to give this to you, so I humbly request that you accept it."

The staff member must have guessed the gist of the situation, whether by intuition or from experience. Shoko reluctantly accepted the bag and made her way to the station.

The announcement for Sakasegawa rang out, and when the train slowed the young woman who had been sitting beside the young man stood up.

"The next time we meet, we should have a drink. I prefer beer in a glass mug rather than in a can."

The guy looked doubtful.

"The central library. You go there a lot, don't you? So then, next time we meet."

And with a rhythm in her step, she alighted from the train—

There was a moment of indecision. Then he leaped off the train and rushed after her, bounding up the staircase.

Apparently they weren't a couple—yet.

"Too bad," Shoko murmured softly.

The start of new love, always a pleasure to see—but the timing was cruel.

She began to feel sullied by the curse she may have cast over the bridal couple's happiness. The groom's reputation was already substantially diminished within the company, but it would be almost impossible to change jobs in this recession, while the bride didn't have the luxury to be able to just quit, even though her female colleagues were giving her the cold shoulder at the office.

Gossip may last seventy-five days, as the saying goes, but so long as Shoko still worked there—the ever-present victim of their shocking behavior—the scandal would never go away.

She would never quit. To do so would make it too easy on them. This determination was warping her, she knew that, but the logical advice that there was no use holding a grudge or putting a curse on them didn't ease Shoko's mind either.

One thing she was sure of: to quit now would only mean accepting defeat. And so, at the very least, she would hold out until the quiet type took her maternity leave (she was also the type who probably wouldn't come back to work anyway).

An older woman and a young girl came in from the next car, in search of empty seats, and the young girl pointed at Shoko, exclaiming happily, "A bride!"

In that instant, tears spilled down Shoko's cheeks.

*That's right, I wanted to be a bride, alongside the man I'd been with for five years. Our love wasn't born from inertia and compromise. It was like that young man who just leaped off the train and the young woman he was chasing after. My ex may have been a bit unreliable, but he was kind and I loved him. I thought his jitters were only temporary, while we were planning our wedding, but ultimately his unreliability is what ruined us.*

*I never wanted things to end like this, with my illusions about him completely shattered by that conniving woman. Because when she married him, she didn't just steal him away from me, she trampled upon and ruined the five years I had with him. I was so wounded, it felt all I could do was simply hand him over.*

*I'm no bride, young lady.*

*I dressed up like a bride in this white dress so that I could put a curse on their life together.*

# Sakasegawa Station

*My, how adorable!*

Tokié's eyes crinkled at the sight of the couple who were standing in the middle of the staircase.

The young man was speaking earnestly to the long-haired young woman who was carrying a tote bag featuring the Disney character beloved by Tokié's granddaughter, who was with her today.

"If you'd like to have a drink, how about today? Are you free now?"

He must have run up this long staircase, because he sounded breathless.

"But, uh, not if you have a boyfriend . . ."

"I don't," the young woman replied cheerfully, smiling at him. "In fact, I'm looking for one. So your invitation is quite welcome."

"OK, great!"

"I'd love to."

From the corner of her eye, Tokié witnessed this heartwarming scene of budding romance just as her granddaughter called out, "Granny, the train is coming!" before they both stepped quickly down the rest of the stairs. She wasn't so old yet; she could still hustle without worrying about her back or her knees.

She and her granddaughter dashed onto the train and then stopped to catch their breath.

They had even made it with time to spare—the announcement cautioning against last-second boarding had yet to blare from the loudspeaker.

"Nice hustle, Granny!"

Her granddaughter had gotten to be a sassy little thing, though as a grandmother, it would have been immature of Tokié to inform her that had she been alone, there was no doubt she would have still made it—so she refrained.

Her son and his wife wanted to see a movie that day, so Tokié had offered to take care of her granddaughter. The plan had been a trip to the dog park that had opened on what used to be the site of an amusement park, Takarazuka Family Land. It was the perfect destination for her dog-loving granddaughter. Even though Tokié didn't have a dog, they could still take the dogs at the park for a walk. Tokié had also promised that on their way home, they could get off at Sakasegawa, where she would buy the girl a snack and a present at the biggest hundred-yen shop around, which was her granddaughter's favorite (likely because her pestering was more successful there than at a regular store).

"Weren't they cute today?"

Her granddaughter was talking about the Welsh corgis. Tokié hadn't let on how much she herself loved dogs and that she was actually more knowledgeable about breeds than her granddaughter.

There were no empty seats, but it looked like there might be some in the next car, so the two of them moved on, hand in hand.

"Granny, did you bring découpage again for today?"

"Yes, I did, a new project."

"My mom says I don't need any more."

Her daughter-in-law had yet to realize that children didn't keep things to themselves. Although it would have been even worse if she had been using her daughter to convey the not-so-subtle message.

"I'll still leave them with you even if you don't need them."

Tokié's son and his wife were not shy about using her as a babysitter, although over the years since her husband passed away, they seemed to have forgotten to even mention the prospect of Tokié living with them. For her part, Tokié hadn't the slightest interest in making her way into a home where she felt unwelcome, so she didn't mention it either.

Curiously, their relationship was not strained. She stayed over with them in their condo sometimes, and they all came over to stay at Tokié's home other times.

Tokié's late husband had left her the house, for which the mortgage had been fully paid off, along with a tidy sum of money, and when she died, presumably Tokié's son—as their only child—and his wife would inherit these from her.

It's not that she didn't worry about whether she would need care, but she had taken out private insurance for this possibility and was conscientious about her diet and exercise. As Tokié got older, it was perfectly natural for her to hope for a sudden death, one that didn't create a burden for anyone.

She figured that so long as she was still living on her own, she was entitled to one last selfish wish. Something she'd been wanting since her husband passed away.

While there was still time, she wanted to have a dog.

Being obligated to walk a dog would be good for her health.

Even if she were unable to care for it, her granddaughter loved dogs, and with the inheritance, her son and his wife could manage to look after one little dog.

Tokié was pondering all of this as they moved to the next car, where, standing by the door, they saw a woman in a snow-white dress, looking just like a runaway bride. She was quite a beauty, though the look on her face gave the impression that she had just stabbed someone.

Her granddaughter may love dogs, but she was also of the age where she adored princesses and brides and frilly lace dresses, so she pointed at the woman and exclaimed, "A bride!"

Just then, tears flowed down the woman's cheeks.

A grown-up could intuit that there must be extenuating circumstances. By the woman's feet, there was a wedding favor bag from the Takarazuka Hotel, a top-notch hotel in the area. Anyone with common sense and courtesy knew that you didn't wear an ostentatious white dress when invited to a wedding.

Furthermore, a dress as beautiful as that must have cost at least a hundred thousand yen. Judging from those tears in response to Tokié's granddaughter, the woman appeared perfectly intelligent—not the type to commit an unintentional gaffe.

Her granddaughter seemed utterly enthralled, and immediately took the spare seat next to where the woman was standing.

There was not quite enough space beside her granddaughter, which made it preferable for Tokié to stand in front of her, hanging on to the strap.

Her granddaughter was staring inquisitively at the tearful woman. For better or worse, the girl was curious about everything, so it was only a matter of time before she started asking why the bride was crying.

Tokié figured there was a better chance of avoiding embarrassment for the woman by preemptively engaging her in conversation. Her granddaughter had enough discipline to know that she wasn't supposed to butt in to grown-ups' conversations.

"Was it a successful incursion?"

It seemed to take a moment for the woman to register Tokié's question.

"Are you speaking to me?"

"Yes, I asked you a question."

Tokié might like to think that her blunt way of speaking was straightforward and natural, but the woman seemed to have taken it as critical.

"You must think I'm ridiculous—a woman wearing a white dress like this and carrying a wedding favor."

"Don't take it the wrong way—I'm not criticizing you at all. If anything, you might very well think I'm the one who's ridiculous. A nosy old lady asking a stranger whether her revenge was successful."

The woman looked like she'd been caught off guard, but then she chuckled.

"I'm not sure whether I was successful or not. It's possible I may have only brought them closer together, in their hatred toward me. But I hope that when they think of their wedding, the two of them remember me. I won't let it be the happiest day of their lives. I want to make their wedding a day they'd rather forget."

The woman had been enunciating her words, but then her tone seemed to relax.

"I'm a wronged woman. While I was in the midst of planning my wedding, that hussy took advantage of his jitters to lure him away. It was calculated—once she was pregnant, she came to him, weeping and helpless."

"There have and always will be devious women like that. What a tale of woe."

"That's a strange response," said the woman. "Usually, I'd expect to hear that no matter how much of a grudge I have, putting a curse on my ex is simply not done in polite society. Especially from someone your age."

Tokié replied, "You'd have to be a saint to have that caliber of a thing done to you and *not* put a curse on him. So long as you have the wherewithal and you're certain you won't regret it, no doubt you'll feel much better for striking back."

Her gaze drifted to the landscape outside the window. The houses lining the railway were all old and shabby.

"One must be prepared to take on and atone for the curse, in and of itself. You did it because you feel deeply wounded, and so a stranger's rebuke, no matter how accurate, won't shake your resolve. But I'm nothing more than a nosy bystander."

". . . I'm prettier than the bride."

"No doubt you are."

*Were that not the case, you never would have attempted such an incursion.*

"When they came around to my table, the bride turned to the groom with a fiendish look. She saw that he was looking at me. Seeing me, more beautiful than in all the five years we were together. Ten years from now, when she's a tatty old housewife, worn out from housework and raising kids, I hope he remembers how I looked today. Even when *I'm* worn out, I'm sure I'll age better—and I hope he remembers the woman he could have had, the one he let get away. I hope he remembers how the woman he married, on the day that she looked her best, compares to me. And that he is disillusioned by the life he chose so rashly."

She spat out this noxious venom that some might have interpreted as boastful. But the woman who looked as though she had just stabbed someone was herself wounded, unavoidably spattered with the blood of her victims.

"I don't care whether people think I'm arrogant or nasty. I was willing to do whatever it took to put a hex on those two. I wanted to make sure that what ought to have been the finest day of their lives would be jinxed."

"You've got mettle." Tokié nodded and then shifted the conversation. "So, do you work at the same company as the bride and groom?"

"Yes."

"This is unsolicited advice from a nosy bystander, so take it as you like."

The woman listened solemnly.

"For now you can curse them to your heart's content. Your

mere presence at the office will be humiliating and will surely affect his prospects."

Tokié deliberately didn't mention anything about the bride. Her own life experience told her that there was little chance such a crafty woman would return to work after giving birth—and that in light of the circumstances, she had little motivation to do so. Even having accomplished her scheme to steal another woman's man, it was doubtful she had the grit or the guts to withstand the scornful looks from her colleagues.

"But once you're satisfied with the curse, you ought to quit."

Tokié offered no further explanation, and the woman fell quiet. She seemed to have a good head on her shoulders and to be taking in Tokié's message.

With the groom now saddled with such a clingy partner, relentlessly pursuing the destruction of their life together would backfire, earning her their enduring resentment. The curse would then encumber her for the rest of her life.

Tokié had no idea about the depth or breadth of the woman's love for the man. But she was still young and beautiful—this blow, though painful, was not fatal. She would surely recover, of this Tokié was certain.

"I understand," the woman responded at long last and with seemingly immense sincerity.

"NEXT STOP, OBAYASHI. OBAYASHI."

The station announcement came on, and Tokié offered one more bit of unsolicited advice.

"If I may, consider getting off at Obayashi. You look pale, and Obayashi is a lovely station for a respite."

The woman tilted her head doubtfully but, taking in the

recommendation of a woman with whom she'd just had such a candid exchange in the span of a single stop on the train, she nodded and said, "I think I will do just that."

The train slowed as it pulled into the station.

The doors opened, and a young couple boarded—looking overtly at the woman's stark white dress, so conspicuous on a regular local train.

Tokié's granddaughter called after the woman in white, who had just gotten off.

"Miss, you forgot something."

The woman's shoulders shuddered. Perhaps she had meant to leave it behind. She turned back to retrieve the wedding favor bag.

She smiled stiffly, took the favor bag from the girl, and, with a wave, got off the train again.

"Such a pretty bride, wasn't she!"

Tokié's granddaughter gazed wistfully at the figure in white as the train began to move.

"That was not a bride."

Perhaps the reason for Tokié's dry tone as she corrected her granddaughter had to do with a certain disdain for the real bride of the day.

"A bride does not ride the train by herself. There was no groom, now, was there?"

"Oh, you're right!"

White is not only for brides. In historical dramas, the woman who performs the ox-hour shrine visit wears white. She too is there to lay a curse.

White can encompass celebration as well as malediction and

malice. But perhaps it was not the time to share such information with her granddaughter.

"Did you see her? That was crazy, huh?"

"She was a looker, though."

"C'mon, d'ya really think so?"

The couple who had boarded the train when the woman had gotten off were standing by the opposite door and, sure enough, had started chatting about her, their comments genial but indiscreet.

"She's wearing what looks like a wedding dress, but she's carrying a wedding favor."

"What's so strange about that?"

"Ugh, I swear, guys have NO clue how to behave at special occasions. It's majorly tacky for an invited guest to wear white to a wedding. Especially a dress as fancy as that. Something's gotta be up with that."

This assessment by the girl in the couple was spot-on, but Tokié preferred for her granddaughter not to hear the conversation. And despite how young she still was, Ami had noticed that the couple were discussing the woman who had just left the train. She sat quite still, pretending to be well behaved while listening attentively to what they were saying. Even if she didn't fully understand, soon enough she'd be able to guess that the girl in the couple was not saying nice things.

"Ami."

As soon as Tokié called her name, her granddaughter looked up. Apparently, even at her age, she knew enough to feel guilty for eavesdropping.

"So, I'm thinking about getting a dog—what do you think?"

"Wow, *really*?!"

The girl's face instantly brightened. Tokié could tell from the sparkle in her eyes that both the woman in the white dress and the couple's conversation about her were already forgotten.

*It's for the best. She's too young to worry about stories like that.*

"I think you should get a golden retriever, Granny!"

"Oh, Ami, I don't have the energy to keep up with such a big dog. Better for me to get a smaller dog."

"You mean like the ones we saw today . . . a corgi?"

"That's right, about that size. But I think a Shiba Inu might be nice."

"Ah, Shiba puppies are so cute!"

Her granddaughter's love for dogs was so complete, she'd support whatever breed Tokié might suggest.

"What about an even smaller one, Granny, like a Chihuahua?"

"Well, personally I'd prefer to get a slightly bigger dog."

After all, she did have the whole house to herself. Whereas a big dog might be too much for her, she'd prefer one with a bit more presence than a Chihuahua.

"I hope you get one soon, Granny! Then I can help you out with dog walks!"

Tokié began a semiserious enumeration of potential dog breeds, including explanations of whichever breeds were unfamiliar to her granddaughter, and these hypothetical dogs seemed to overwrite any memory of the weary-looking quasi-bride.

"But Granny, if you love dogs, how come you've never had one all this time?"

The question caught Tokié off guard—she paused to ponder

why herself. As a child she'd had a number of dogs, and once she was married, they'd had their own house, so there hadn't been any restrictions that would have prevented it—

"Oh! Ah yes, that's right..."

As she recalled the reason—completely forgotten up to this point—Tokié chuckled.

"Gramps didn't like dogs."

"What?"

Back in their day, love marriages were still rare. Tokié's had been an arranged marriage—after being introduced by a matchmaker, she and her suitor's feelings for each other had slowly grown fonder.

One day he gently asked, "Next Sunday, would it be all right for me to come to your house and introduce myself to your parents?" Tokié had no reason to refuse. He was hardworking and good-natured, the kind of person with whom she could imagine spending the rest of her life.

And so it was that on the following Sunday, the man who would be her husband put on his best suit and, with a bouquet of flowers for Tokié in one hand and a bottle of fine sake for her parents in the other, he arrived at her home.

Her parents and brothers gave him a grand welcome, everyone standing at the front door and making a bit of a fuss over him. But there was someone who did not appreciate all this commotion.

The beaming smile on Tokié's future husband's face as he greeted them suddenly changed dramatically.

"Yikes—!"

Oh, no—wondering what had happened, they turned to see

that the family dog, a Kai Ken whose doghouse was right by the entryway, had bitten him on the backside and remained firmly attached.

Though a banquet had been set in the drawing room, Tokié's future husband lowered his trousers in their sitting room—his best suit ruined (of course, fearing for their reputation, Tokié's father would later pay him compensation)—where the doctor, on a house call, daubed the suitor's backside with iodine tincture and remonstrated the family about summoning him for a minor injury they could have treated themselves. Perhaps it was true that the family could have treated the injury themselves, but just who among them would have been appropriate to minister to the exposed backside of the young man chosen for their daughter, who had come there to ask for her hand in marriage? Later in their life together, Tokié would apply medicine to his bites and even hemorrhoids, but at that time, the couple had barely exchanged a kiss.

The suitor somehow managed to get through his proposal, but since it was difficult for him to sit down, he beat a hasty retreat, hardly eating any of the feast. Tokié's mother insisted on packing some of the food for him to take home, but all in all, it was a miserable experience.

Though before all of this, he may have been fine with dogs, he seemed traumatized thereafter and developed a fear of them (and certainly of the Kai Ken breed, a hunting dog with powerful jaws). If they happened to encounter a dog, no matter how small, he would squawk and hide behind Tokié.

And that was why, even after they had their own house, the prospect of having a dog never even occurred to either of them.

Over the last few years since her husband died, Tokié longed to have a dog—it was now or never.

The awful memory of being bitten on the backside before his marriage proposal had scarred her husband to the point that he would cry out if they even crossed paths with a Chihuahua, the sight of which would lead their grown son to tease his father, which would then cause her husband to sulk. Tokié would take note of where there were likely to be dogs and nonchalantly lead them on a detour so as to avoid them. She would take these memories of their life together to her own grave.

*Forgive me, my dear.*

If she got a dog, would that make it difficult for her husband's spirit to return home for the Bon festival and his memorial services? she wondered. *You'll be fine*, she thought. Now that he's a ghost, he'd have no need to avoid dogs, right? She'd put the dog in its cage for the Bon festival. *If you like, you can sit on top of my head.*

She'd just make sure not to get a Kai Ken.

# Obayashi Station

*Just what's so lovely about this station?*

Shoko had gotten off the train at the old lady's recommendation and was taking in her surroundings.

She considered going into the waiting lounge on the same platform, but the windowed, cold-looking interior contained nothing more than a row of hard plastic benches—nothing refined save for the alternating colors of pink and blue. Though air-conditioned in summer and heated in winter, the lounge was still rather rustic. On rainy days, the windows probably fogged up with humidity.

The lavatory was clean, but still, nothing particularly special, and the vending machines looked fairly ordinary too.

Baffled, she headed toward the ticket gate when—

A tiny tailcoat whizzed by, followed by a cacophony of chirping from above.

Shoko looked up to see a swallow's nest, with a clutch of baby swallows leaning out over the sides.

The parent bird shoveled food into the chicks' mouths, before flying off again in a rush, as the same ruckus rose up from the other side.

She turned around to see another nest. Looking about, she counted three while an endless chorus of baby swallows swelled amid the fluttering wings of their parents.

Under each nest, a cradle had been crudely fashioned. And beneath the cradle located just inside the ticket gate, she spotted a notice written in vivid brushstrokes:

*We have returned again this year. Please excuse our commotion and kindly look after us until our fledglings leave the nest.*

A message that would melt even the toughest heart. It must have been written by someone who worked at the station.

Signs calling attention to swallows' nests weren't uncommon, but the ones Shoko usually encountered were to warn about the birds' droppings. She didn't ever recall one that played at being a humorous greeting from the swallows themselves.

She had bought a ticket that allowed her to go as far as Umeda, but she decided to have a look around first. It was such a tiny station, there wasn't even a space for drop-offs. Instead, pedestrians came and went along a gently sloping, forked path that was paved in asphalt on one side and brick on the other.

She exited through the ticket gate and headed down the asphalt path to the point where the brick path veered suddenly to the left. There were a lot of parked bicycles, and as she started down the brick path, she noticed a mini-supermarket and, beyond that, a drugstore.

Under an eave of the supermarket was a white umbrella, hanging upside down by its handle.

*What could that be for?*

She walked up to it in wonder, then clapped her hands together.

Above the umbrella that hung from the soffit lay a swallow's nest, with the canopy of the inverted umbrella positioned to catch bird droppings.

Shoko couldn't help but express her awe at this innovation to the security guard, an older man, who was making sure the bicycles were in order.

"How thoughtful!" she said.

The security guard, whom she guessed to be a part-timer who had taken this job after reaching retirement age, turned and regarded Shoko with a dubious gaze. He appeared not to have heard what she'd said.

"What a good idea!" Speaking a bit louder, Shoko pointed to the umbrella hanging upside down. This time he seemed to have understood.

"Oh, yes, that. We mustn't take down the swallows' nests. They travel such a great distance, they're auspicious birds. But when they build their nest here, what can we do? Customers will get covered with droppings. So we all came up with this idea."

*Obayashi is a lovely station.*

Shoko finally understood what the old lady on the train had meant by those words.

A lovely station and what seemed like a lovely town (although it was so small that calling it a town seemed like a stretch).

It made her want to buy something from this store that hung

an umbrella from its eaves in order to honor both the swallows and their customers. Come to think of it, she had barely eaten anything at the wedding reception, and now she was a bit peckish. There was a bench out front too, so perhaps she would treat herself to a little something to eat and some tea to go with it?

Shoko bowed to the security guard and went inside. At the front was an array of vegetables at bargain prices—she was tempted to buy some but thought better of it; she didn't feel like carrying them all the way home.

It didn't take long to make her way around the entire store, but for such a small space, it had an impressive selection. The mini-market was modest in scale but extremely resourceful with its stock, plus it stayed open late at night. Particularly convenient for someone who lived alone. You could quickly grow tired of eating meals from the convenience store. *To have a store like this in the neighborhood would make grocery shopping fun, even if both of you worked . . .* No sooner did her mind wander than she remembered how that opportunity was now lost to her, and she felt a sudden pang in her chest.

There was an assortment of prepared foods near the register: bento meals and such, as well as a basket piled up with onigiri. Except these were not typical convenience-store-style packaged items—the rice was studded with pickles, rolled by hand into balls and wrapped in cellophane. Charmed by their homeyness, Shoko selected an ume-shiso onigiri along with a bottle of green tea, and paid for them.

Today's clear skies had offered a break in the rainy season, and the bench felt pleasantly warm. Without a second thought about creating wrinkles in her dress, she finally sat down, her stubborn insistence on standing while on the train now evaporated.

The onigiri looked simple and unpretentious, like the ones her mother used to roll and press into shape with all the requisite maternal care. Shoko savored it, chewing slowly and washing it down with the tea. That single rice ball was enough to quell her hunger.

Shoko threw the empty wrapper and bottle in the trash bin, and then called out to the security guard she'd spoken to earlier.

"Excuse me."

"What can I do for you?" the security guard responded affably, perhaps still feeling pleased about her praise for the umbrella idea.

"Is there a store around here where I can buy some clothes?"

This mini-market didn't have a clothing section, so she figured it wouldn't be rude to ask him.

The security guard cocked his head, confounded. Perhaps it was unlikely he'd know about any local women's boutiques.

Eventually, though, he pointed to a large supermarket that faced the sloping path toward the station.

"I think they have a ladies' clothing section in there."

Compared to this cozy little store, the building looked huge—there was no way of missing it.

Shoko thanked the man and bowed, then started down the slope.

Shoko in her stark white dress received a few nonjudgmental looks. This town had an everyday feel to it, and most of the people coming and going in the early afternoon along this sloping path were dressed casually. Her dress stood out conspicuously.

There was no point in rushing now, so she strolled down the street toward the supermarket that the security guard had pointed out.

∽

In the four-level supermarket, the ladies' clothing section was not far from the escalator to the second floor. As she browsed around, Shoko was aware of people's gaze upon her, still without any sense of meanness. The clothing on offer was targeted at older women, or else young housewives—it wasn't the kind of place where Shoko would usually shop.

She selected an acceptable pair of trousers and a knit top, which she brought to the register.

"Excuse me, I'd like to wear these right away. Could you cut the tags off so that I can change into them in the fitting room?"

Clad in a navy uniform, the female employee gave Shoko a look. After showing her to the fitting room, she lingered outside while Shoko changed, as if suspecting she was up to some kind of clever trick. Even if that wasn't the case, clearly Shoko's dress had been noticed.

Having changed out of it, Shoko stuffed the dress into her plastic bag, making the package as compact as possible and tying off the handles.

She pulled back the curtain and came out of the fitting room, and when the employee saw what was crammed into the transparent plastic bag, she exclaimed with surprise, "But, miss, your dress . . ."

She was obviously concerned that the outfit Shoko had

changed out of was much more expensive than what she had just purchased.

"It's fine," Shoko said as she slipped her high heels back on and picked up her handbag. These dressy accessories were a bit incongruous with her now-casual clothing, but not quite enough to attract attention. "Well then . . ." Shoko bowed her head as she departed, leaving the employee standing dumbfounded.

Once outside, Shoko tossed the bag stuffed with the dress into a garbage bin.

Considering what she had spent on it, perhaps she ought to have gotten rid of it at a consignment shop, but the dress was tainted with Shoko's grudge and with the successful incursion into the wedding reception of the woman who had slept with her fiancé. Shoko wouldn't want to inflict that misfortune on anyone else, so her better judgment had prevailed.

And anyway, it would have been a futile effort to recoup a trifling sum. The hundred thousand yen she paid for the dress was the price of her incursion—and it had been money well spent. She needn't worry about the shoes and the bag—those were things she'd already had in her wardrobe.

These thoughts cleared her head.

It was a pain to have to carry the wedding favor all the way home, but those items would need to go into the recycling, so that couldn't be helped.

Having come all the way here, she figured she might as well have a good look around, so she set off walking again, heading for a narrow, bustling street when—

*Whoosh!*

From the eaves of a boxed-lunch shop and a beauty parlor nestled along the street, three swallows swooped low, like a fluttering flash. A closer look revealed that the eaves of these shops were also home to nests.

Of course, Shoko had seen swallows before, but it had been a long time since she'd had such an up-close-and-personal encounter with their nesting behavior and swooping flight patterns.

This town was far from sleepy—rather, it was as lively as one could expect for a population of its size. But for migrating swallows, it clearly seemed like a fine place to build a nest and to raise their young.

*Indeed—a lovely station in a lovely town.*

It was just as the old woman had said.

Though since Shoko was unfamiliar with the area, best not to venture too far. She'd do a loop around the supermarket and then head back to the station. The trees lining the road around the supermarket's parking lot looked to be in full bloom.

They appeared to be the same variety of tree but in different colors, practically bursting with flowers in alternating white and pink. She was filled with awe—even the landscaping was a delight.

She had made it almost all the way around the supermarket, so she continued walking under those pink and white blossoms as she headed toward the station.

Passing a drugstore along the way, she decided to pick up a travel packet of facial cleansing wipes.

She walked idly on toward the station. Despite the narrowness of the streets, there was a steady stream of cars coming and going—it seemed the town was thriving.

*It'd be nice to live here someday . . .* Even Shoko was surprised by the thought that flitted through her mind. The location *did* seem unexpectedly convenient and livable.

Slowly—and reluctantly—she arrived back at the path to the station.

*How boring to take the same road*, she thought as she bypassed the slope she had come down earlier, choosing instead to take the next street that was also in the direction of the tracks. Sure enough, the train's pantograph came into view. The end of this street connected with the forked brick path outside the ticket gate. She could see the turnstiles ahead.

She climbed back up the gentle slope, and as she hovered in front of the ticket machine, she made another pleasant discovery.

The sides of the machines were decorated with art that was clearly the work of small hands, celebrating the Tanabata Star Festival.

> These decorations were made and donated by students from XX elementary school. May the lovers Princess Orihime (the Vega star) and Hikoboshi (the Altair star) be reunited again this year.

From the looks of it, this must have been the youngest students—rather than the entire elementary school—who decided among themselves to make these decorations and offer them to the station employees, who had accepted them graciously, as adults are wont to do.

Nevertheless, how many grown-ups nowadays would respectfully display children's clumsy decorations? Especially when they weren't those children's teachers or parents.

Shoko bought another ticket for Umeda, and after passing through the ticket gate, she called out to the person in the booth.

"Excuse me . . ."

"Yes, what is it?" A salt-and-pepper-haired station employee emerged from the booth and responded amiably.

Shoko reached into the wedding favor bag and pulled out the ornamental cookie gift.

"Perhaps you and your colleagues would enjoy these?" she said, setting the cookies on the counter.

The man looked a bit puzzled, and before he could offer an excuse, Shoko continued:

"I was invited to a little event, and these were the favor that was handed out. I have a condition that prevents me from eating sweets. These cookies are from the hotel, and it would be a waste to throw them away, so if you're willing to take them, I'd be grateful."

In contrast to her dress, bought for the express purpose of her incursion, these cookies were blameless. What's more, they had been baked at the hotel with the sincerest of intentions. Relinquishing them was a matter of convenience for Shoko—as long as someone else ate them, she would avoid the guilt of letting them go to waste.

"You say you have a condition—are you diabetic?" The station employee looked concerned. "What a pity, you're so young. Isn't there someone at home who might enjoy them?"

## The Passengers on the Hankyu Line

"I live alone. And I was so happy to see that sign over there, I'd like to do something for the station workers before I go. As a sort of refreshment." Shoko pointed toward the notice about the swallows.

The man scratched his head.

"They come here every year, and they're so adorable. I'm the one who built the cradles, but I enlisted someone with far better penmanship for the sign."

"It's lovely."

As Shoko bowed and moved along, the station employee picked up the fancy cookies from the Takarazuka Hotel.

"Thank you very much! I will tell the person who penned the sign!" The man bowed deeply.

When she got to the platform, the train was about to pull in, but Shoko stepped into the lavatory.

She took a look at her party makeup with fresh eyes—it really looked like war paint.

*Make me gorgeous.* With the wedding in mind, for the first time in her life she'd had her makeup done by a professional. *I want to be the most beautiful I've ever looked.* The makeup artist was highly skilled, and indeed, Shoko's glamorous appearance had upstaged the bride.

The look on that woman's face when she saw Shoko. As if she'd seen a demon, or karma incarnate.

Wringing that look out of her had been well worth the cost of a professional makeup artist. In fact, it was priceless.

Her work was done.

Shoko pulled out the wipes she had just bought and began to clean her face. It took five sheets to fully unmake the elaborately applied splendor.

She redid her makeup with the products she had on hand. A natural look this time.

Apart from her somewhat drab spur-of-the-moment outfit, she looked almost like her usual self.

The incursion was over.

Shoko could not yet wholly let go of her resentment, but her thrust had hit the mark. And she had no regrets.

*When will my time come?*

It was thanks to the old woman, who had struck up a conversation with her on the train, that Shoko could even begin to ponder that question.

# Nigawa Station

"I'm telling you!"

Misa laughed as she explained the same thing over again, one more time.

They were talking about the woman in the white dress who had gotten off at Obayashi Station.

Misa wore a smile, but inwardly she was rather irritated.

"There's something weird about being invited to a wedding and showing up in a white dress."

"What the hell? S'long as you're invited, you're a guest, and guests can wear what they like."

Her boyfriend Katsuya's counterargument wasn't much of one, and they were just going around in circles.

"Fine, sure, the guests are part of the event on the wedding day, but there's no question that the bride is the star of the show. The bride and groom are supposedly the hosts, and the guests are there to celebrate them. Everybody knows that white is the bride's color, so people with any common sense don't wear white."

"Who says what's common sense?"

"Common sense is just stuff you know, it's not like there's anyone who decides it." Misa let out a sigh. "Come on, you wouldn't show up to a wedding dressed like that, would you?"

Katsuya's look that day was baggy hip-hop streetwear.

"What, now you're complaining about the way I dress?"

"No, that's not what I meant! Just that there's an appropriate time and place for everything."

*Ugh, why do my conversations with Katsuya always go like this? It's not like what I'm saying is so out there or anything . . .*

"If you're a girl, you have to be careful what you wear, even if it's a white shawl. You don't want to upset the bride, of course, nor do you want everyone else to think you're clueless."

Katsuya snickered through his nose. "Girls waste their time on so much bullshit. You're a perfect example."

They'd been dating for about a year, so she was familiar with his cursing, but every so often he'd spew some inexcusable criticism or abuse that went too far. And whenever this happened, it wasn't Misa's nature to remain silent.

Though it was only afterward that she remembered how much irritation it created.

"So you think you know more about weddings than I do? You mentioned you recently went to an older friend's wedding, right? Are you sure you RSVP'd properly?"

"'Course I did—all you do is just send that thing back."

"So how did you fix the return address on the front of the response card?"

Katsuya's complexion changed—a quirk of his that happened when someone pointed out something he didn't know.

"Don't tell me you just sent it back as is?"

Misa was still annoyed about Katsuya's rude comment, and so now her tone turned mean as she grilled him. Katsuya still didn't respond, and his silence made it clear that was exactly what he had done.

"It's impolite to return the response card addressed to you with the honorific 'sama' still intact, so you cross it out with two diagonal lines, to be humble, and write 'from' before your own name. Then you cross out the 'from' in front of the sender's name and change their title to 'sama'—that's just good manners."

Katsuya sulked in silence.

"On the other side, you can't just circle 'will attend' and fill in your name and address. Again, you have to cross out the honorific and make sure you also cross out 'will not attend.'"

She chose not to mention the additional courtesy of writing in "accepts with pleasure" or some other nicety—that'd be far too much to expect of Katsuya. It had been her intention to stop there, but she couldn't help herself. Part of it was payback for his nasty comment; part of it was just her being bossy.

"... Of course you also have to make sure you cross out the honorifics where you fill in your name and address—"

Katsuya interrupted her lecture by suddenly kicking the train door that he was leaning against. Misa flinched. Katsuya's eyes were glassy. She looked around anxiously, and indeed, the sound had drawn stares from everyone in the car.

A young girl seated opposite was looking over with eyes wide. So was the woman beside her, who appeared to be her grandmother.

Katsuya, no doubt aware of the other passengers' attention, kicked the door again, harder this time.

"You think you're such hot shit because you know all that, huh?"

*Fuck.*

At least they weren't someplace private, like at Katsuya's apartment, where he lived alone . . .

Someplace where he'd hit her.

"S-sorry. It's not that I think I know everything, it's just . . . it's social etiquette, so I thought it'd be good for you to know about it too—"

"You makin' fun of me?! You think you're hot shit because you know all this etiquette crap, so you can lecture me?!"

He kicked the door a third time.

The little girl started to whimper. Not because she thought it was directed at her but because the sound of the door being kicked so roughly and the abuse being hurled so brazenly in public was scary for a child.

*Oh, I'm sorry, little girl. It's this big girl's fault.*

Just as Misa was thinking this, Katsuya clucked his tongue and muttered, more quietly this time, "Shut up, you little brat!"

*Wait a minute, jerk. You're* the one who made her cry.

But she didn't dare say that to him—he was so worked up, he might actually slap her in front of everyone.

"NEXT STOP, NIGAWA. NIGAWA."

As the announcement came over the speaker, the girl and grandmother pair stood up.

Katsuya also turned to face the door that was about to open, and Misa walked quickly after him.

"Wait, we're not getting off here! We were gonna go to the real estate broker in Nishi-Kita to look for a place."

"I don't feel like it anymore, because of you."

*Because of you.* His emphasis on that phrase was spiteful.

"I'd rather go bet on the horses, even if there isn't a big race today. If you wanna look for an apartment, go by yourself."

Nigawa serves the Hanshin Racecourse, and on in-season weekends, the station teems with horse racing spectators. So many pedestrians throng to the racecourse on major race days that the crosswalk signal can't handle the flow of traffic, so they built a passageway that offers direct access from the ticket gate to the racecourse for people who arrive by train. In the opposite direction, there is a traditional shopping district that leads to a peaceful, quiet residential area. The difference from one side of the station to the other could not be starker.

Katsuya had no interest in horse racing. He only ever went along if his friends invited him, and even then only for the big races. For him to get off here, that could only be interpreted as Katsuya being hurtful to Misa.

As the grandmother-granddaughter pair stood waiting to get off, the older woman was trying to soothe the girl, who was still sniffling.

Katsuya made a point of mouthing the word "bitch" at the woman. The implication being that this too was because of Misa.

"Hey, I'm sorry, it's my fault. I'll stop. Will you change your mind and come to the broker with me?"

The train came to a halt and the doors opened. Misa tried to prevent Katsuya from getting off, but instead she got dragged along.

"Eek!"

Misa came close to tripping over onto the platform, but Katsuya didn't even turn around; he just shook off her hand and hustled over to the ticket gate.

Any impulse to chase after him vanished, and Misa just watched him go.

*Ugh, how did we get to this point?*

They argued when they were out on a date, when they were at home in Katsuya's apartment and, if she wasn't careful, even after they'd just done it.

*Just what was wrong?* Why was it that the most insignificant comment would always escalate into a full-blown argument? Things would go beyond the point of no return, and if they were at his place, he'd hit her, or if they were out, he'd lose his temper and walk off. Misa had lost count of the times she'd had to make her own way home in tears.

And yet, when he had been in a good mood, he'd suggested they live together, rather than each living alone, since it would save them both money on rent.

I think you and I will get along just fine, he'd said.

Still, whenever his anger flared, he was relentless. No matter how Misa pleaded and cried, no matter how much she apologized, it had no effect. Once an argument had begun, it wasn't over until he decided it was.

She and Katsuya had been the first ones off the train, and the other passengers stepped off after them. By now Misa was used to the pitiful stares.

The sound of someone blowing their nose echoed loudly. Misa couldn't help but turn to look—it was the same pair from before. The elderly lady was helping the little girl clean herself up after crying.

"I'm sorry for making your granddaughter cry." Misa couldn't help but offer an apology.

With a practiced hand, the old lady briskly disposed of the tissue and uttered flatly, "That good-for-nothing."

It took a moment for Misa to realize that the woman's offhand comment was in reference to Katsuya.

The shock of it was a rude awakening to Misa—the fact that she was dating a guy whom a total and complete stranger felt compelled to dismiss aloud as a good-for-nothing.

"Have you thought about getting rid of him? For all he puts you through."

The old lady spoke in a frank tone as she took the hand of her granddaughter, no longer crying, and descended the staircase toward the opposite exit.

Misa watched their retreating figures until they were no longer visible, then trudged along the platform to a nearby bench, where she took a seat.

*Why am I dating such a jerk?*

An insignificant comment escalated into a full-blown argument, and in his anger, he saw nothing wrong with yelling at her in public; if no one was around, he became violent, without any concern that he might actually injure her.

Their relationship had begun when he first chatted her up. Katsuya was a good-looking guy, and Misa had been flattered when he had struck up a conversation with her. She agreed to go to a café with him.

As they talked, it turned out that they both attended universities along the same railway line, and what's more, while they had both grown up in the Kansai region, the commute to campus from home was too arduous, so they were both living on their own.

Things progressed quickly from there. They exchanged mobile phone numbers that same day, and within a month, their relationship was already to the point where they were staying over at each other's apartments.

If she were being honest, everything in their relationship *had* happened pretty quickly, but Katsuya had been much sweeter when they first started dating.

*But when had things gotten this bad?*

At some point Misa had taken on the chores at Katsuya's, so she warmed to the idea of moving in together because she was fed up with doing the housework both at her place and his.

*That's right—it didn't even take a year for him to make me into a perfectly devoted housewife.*

It was because she took pleasure in making him happy. But it wasn't long before he got used to it and eventually took it for granted that she'd keep doing it. Katsuya didn't even bother tidying up after himself in his own apartment, and he'd let his laundry pile up—he'd blithely call her up to say, "Come over, I'm almost out of clean underwear."

At first, when she'd told him that she wasn't his housekeeper and that he should do it himself, he had mumbled and nodded in acquiescence, but it wasn't long before that response from her would elicit a sour mood. The endless arguments had started up around that time too, and caught in a nonstop loop of fighting,

Misa gave up and basically just went over to Katsuya's every week to keep up with the chores.

Out of this exasperation came the search for an apartment.

But then, no matter how hard Misa tried, there would be incidents like what happened today. She hated to admit it to herself—that despite how hard she tried, her boyfriend showed absolutely no consideration for her.

And on top of that...

*I'm not even living with this guy yet, and he doesn't give a second thought to hitting me during a fight. If I move in with him, I'll have no place to run to get away!*

"I wanna go home."

Misa stood up from the bench and walked over to a boarding spot on the platform. It would be several minutes until the next train.

Previously, she would have called Katsuya repeatedly, and when he didn't answer, she would have left numerous apologetic messages. It would not have been unusual for her to stand by the ticket gate and wait for him to reappear.

But from this newfound place of detached composure, she was able to question the necessity of clinging to a guy like him. What was more...

*My mother would be so sad if she knew that my boyfriend hits me.*

This thought had never even crossed her mind before. And now it made her feel like such an undutiful daughter. It wasn't only her mother whom she had let down but her entire family—and her friends too. Everyone would be so sad if they knew.

It had not taken long for the no-nonsense advice proffered by the old lady as she went on her way to snap Misa back to her senses. Even Misa found it odd how quickly she'd been able to relinquish her attachment to Katsuya.

It'd be a few hours before he returned from the racetrack. Misa had a key to his apartment, and that would give her plenty of time to collect her things. Last night had been one of the rare occasions when Katsuya stayed over at her apartment in Obayashi—it would be the last. She would send the few items of his that were at her place to him by delivery service.

Misa knew their breakup would be complicated, but she was prepared for any mudslinging. Luckily, because it was usually Katsuya who summoned her to his place, she hadn't given him a key. If worse came to worst, she would call a friend or even the police...

*Now I guess I should send him one last message.*

She thought about it for a moment and then swiftly tapped out a text on her phone:

I've had enough of your shit. Goodbye.

She saved it as a draft—she would fire off that message once she was safely back home in her own apartment—and then she boarded the train that had slid into the platform.

# Koto'en Station

Misa swayed about on the train, with the resolute intention of firing off the message saved on her phone, tucked away inside her bag.

There were a few available seats dotted around, but standing suited her current mood.

"*That good-for-nothing. Have you thought about getting rid of him? For all he puts you through.*"

*It didn't even take a year for him to make me into a perfectly devoted housewife . . .*

*He doesn't give a second thought to hitting me during a fight. If I move in with him . . .*

*My mother would be so sad if she knew that my boyfriend hits me.*

In a moment of decisiveness, she had composed her breakup message, but it only took another moment for Misa to waver.

She had intended to take advantage of Katsuya's absence to retrieve her things from his apartment, and then retreat to her own place . . .

*But he's nice when he's in a decent mood, and he has other good qualities . . .*

*Plus he's pretty good-looking.*

Her friends were always green with envy whenever she displayed photos of the two of them on her phone. "Your boyfriend is so-o cute! Misa, you're so lucky!" they'd say. It was something Misa had taken pride in, and it pained her to think of losing that cachet.

This too made her feel ashamed, that she'd falter over such a thing.

As she idly watched the residential landscape pass before her eyes, the train stopped at the next station, Koto'en.

Koto'en is the nearest station to a well-known private university in Kansai, which means that regardless of whether it is a weekday, weekend or holiday, many of the passengers here seem to be students.

The group of female college students who got on each had a lacrosse stick propped on their shoulder—maybe they were on their way to a scrimmage? A young guy, with kind of a punk style, the drone from his headphones audible, had his nose buried in a daunting-looking textbook.

This university was leagues above the women's college where Misa went, and of course the one Katsuya attended didn't even rate.

Among the passengers who boarded were also a number of high school girls in uniform; they must have had Saturday class. They were laughing boisterously. They seemed utterly carefree, without a thought for the future that lay ahead of them.

*I used to be like them, not so many years ago*, Misa thought. The sound of their cheerful, lighthearted laughter made her a little jealous.

The high school girls occupied the empty space near Misa, grabbing on to the hanging straps and chattering away exuberantly.

"Hey, Et-chan, so your boyfriend is like super older, huh?"

Misa's ears automatically perked up at this cheeky comment—how much of an age difference made him "super older"? she wondered. The girl who appeared to be Et-chan, who also seemed a bit more grown up than the others, waved her hand to deflect the comment. "No, he isn't!"

Et-chan went on to explain: "He's only two years out of university. He has an early birthday, so he's young for his school year—he's a mere five years older than me."

The fact that, at her age, she considered a gap of five years "mere" showed she was one of the more mature ones among her friendship group.

"What? I can't imagine dating a guy with a real job! I mean, if he were older but still in school, I'd get that." The girl who said this was elbowed by one of the others.

"Yeah, but now that we're seniors, we're the oldest. And if we don't go on to college, there's not much chance of going out with an upperclassman."

"Huh, guess you're right. But is it fun to be with a working guy?"

"Yeah, but . . ." Et-chan tilted her head. "It seems like you've all got the wrong idea. A guy can still be clueless, even if he has a job. My boyfriend definitely falls into that category."

One of the girls gasped in disbelief. "Aren't older guys supposed to be dependable and have their shit together?"

From Misa's perspective, this girl seemed like the type who

entertained a certain fantasy about older guys, though Misa was one to talk, since she herself was not quite an adult yet either.

"No way! At least, not my boyfriend! I mean, he just recently started living on his own, and he calls me in the middle of the night, crying for help!"

"Eh? What happened?!"

This girl, Et-chan, was quite the storyteller. All of her friends were hanging on her every word—and Misa was too. *In what kind of scenario does a grown man call up his high-school-age girlfriend in the middle of the night to beg for help?*

"So I was like, 'What's the matter?' and he goes, 'I can't get the iron to work.'"

Her captive audience squealed with laughter. The surrounding passengers began to shoot annoyed looks in the girls' direction, but they seemed completely unbothered—in fact, they didn't even seem to notice—and even Misa was tempted to break into a smile.

"Now, I have to admit that my mom does all the ironing for me, and the only time I've ever done it is in home economics class. Plus, my boyfriend hasn't even told me what it is he's trying to iron. He's already like, 'What temperature should I set it at? And what does it mean by "steam"?' He's way ahead of himself!"

"So true!"

"Then I asked him what he wanted to iron and he said, 'A shirt.' But there are all different kinds of shirts. So I get out my home economics textbook and I ask him what material it is, and he's like, 'Huh? How am I supposed to know that?!' I tell him it's written on the tag, and he goes, 'What tag?'"

The girls erupted into more squeals and high-pitched laughter. Misa's shoulders quivered with a suppressed giggle. The looks from the other passengers in their car grew sterner—but rather than giving them the side-eye, thought Misa, they'd be better off listening to the conversation and having a laugh.

"There's no use being angry and he's about to lose it, so I tell him to look for a little cloth tag that should be attached inside the collar or along one of the side seams. He finally finds it, but then..."

*Wait for it*... Misa thought as she continued to eavesdrop. *Here comes the punch line*...

The finish to Et-chan's story was a wallop.

"He says he can't read the kanji! This is a grown man who went through university!"

"What an idiot!"

Et-chan's friends were brutal in their assessment as they howled and chortled, and their laughter gave cover to Misa's audible giggle.

"And then..."

*There's more?!*

"So I ask him to describe what the characters look like over the phone. He goes, 'Part of it is the character for "thread."'"

"That must be the radical!" said one girl.

"How are you supposed to figure it out from just that?" said another.

These girls were all cramming for their entrance exams that year, so their questions were merciless as they gasped with laughter.

"Well, I know how clueless he is, so I take pity on him. I ask him patiently, 'There must be something else next to the character for "thread," right? What does that look like?' and he says, 'It's like the character for "moon."'"

"He must mean the character for 'silk'!"

"Though he still missed the part that's above the character for 'moon'!"

*This story's got multiple punch lines!* Misa couldn't help it anymore and gave in to her laughter, covering her mouth so it wasn't completely obvious that she was listening.

"So then I looked it up in my textbook and helped him figure out how to iron his shirt. But it's a bit outrageous, isn't it? I mean, for a college graduate with a job?"

It *was* outrageous. There was no question. It was inexcusable for a college graduate with a job not to know how to read the tag on his shirt.

"Did you tell him it's the kanji for 'silk'?"

Et-chan nodded. "He was shocked when I told him. You wouldn't believe how shocked he was."

"I wonder if your boyfriend knows the character for 'cotton'? Seems like there might still be some land mines there . . ."

"Oh, wow—I don't know how I'd manage to explain that kanji to him!"

Et-chan's friends laughed again at her deadpan assessment.

"Then, well, I wasn't sure how he'd take it coming from me, but I kind of told him off over the phone. I said that even though he always uses a computer and hardly ever has to write things out by himself, at some point not knowing kanji is gonna bite him in the backside. I told him he better study up. And he was like, 'I know, you're right. I'll get myself some kanji drills.'

Honestly, I feel like I ought to make him take a reading aptitude test."

It was cruelly amusing to imagine a grown-up getting such a talking-to by a high school girl.

"How did you meet him again?"

"Uh, well, that's not important."

For the first time, the effusive Et-chan hesitated.

"You've never told us, we want to hear," one girl said.

"Yeah, tell us!" said another.

Et-chan hemmed and hawed, and then she warned them not to laugh before reluctantly confessing, "He chatted me up. At Tsukaguchi, no less."

"Wow, that's random!" Her friends didn't laugh, but their voices exclaimed in unison.

By "random," they meant the location, not the way Et-chan and he had met. Tsukaguchi was a large train station where the Itami Line linked up with the Kobe Line, predominantly known for the big hulking shopping center in front of the station where there was a chain supermarket and a bunch of restaurants. Very mundane.

The majority of patrons were housewives, as students from the nearby women's college or high school only ever shopped at Tsukaguchi by necessity, preferring to go to Osaka or Kobe for their real shopping. It was a totally random location for a pickup spot. In front of Tsukaguchi Station, anyone who might be calling out to passersby was usually soliciting for surveys or a blood drive.

"It was my dad's birthday, you know, and I figured Tsukaguchi was a reasonable place to look for a present for him, so I stopped there on my way home from school."

"There's a Muji at Nishi-Kita, you know." The girl who volunteered this was referring to Nishinomiya-Kitaguchi, one of the terminal stations on the Imazu Line they were on now.

"Why would I buy my dad a present at Muji? Muji's more expensive than you think. And my dad's birthday is in February—winter stuff always costs more. I only had a thousand yen to spend."

"All right, then, so Tsukaguchi makes sense."

Not much love for the dads from these girls.

"Right—? So I got him a scarf that was on sale for only one thousand yen. At Muji, it would cost three times that. They wrapped it up for me, and I was about to head home when someone called out to me in front of the station. He asked if I wanted to go to a café with him, his treat."

*Aw, that sounds just like when Katsuya chatted me up . . .* Misa identified with Et-chan's story.

"Then when I turned around, he saw that I was wearing a uniform. And I saw that he was a salaryman. 'Oops,' he said, and clapped his hand to his head. When we first passed by, all he saw was my face, and then I had on my coat, so from behind, he didn't realize I was wearing a uniform. He was like, 'What should we do? If I take you out, will it be like enjo kosai?' But I don't know the first thing about sugar dating."

"So, not to be rude, but it sounds like he was clueless from the start." One of Et-chan's friends chortled.

"I said that if the cops arrested everyone who was sitting in a café together, it'd keep them pretty busy, wouldn't it? So then he said, why don't we go to a tea shop?"

"Wow, the guy's got a job, so that means he has money. You won't end up at McDonald's."

There was something heartwarming to Misa about how wholesome these high school girls seemed. It would cost less than a thousand yen to treat one of them to cake at a tea shop. Then again, that was Et-chan's entire budget for her father's birthday present.

Her friends finally seemed impressed by the notion of an older guy, one who could offer to treat a girl on a whim without putting a dent in his wallet.

"So, does that mean . . ." one of the girls said, lowering her voice. Misa found herself straining to hear. "Have you done it?"

*Right—girls this age have a lot of superficial knowledge without much actual experience.* Misa smirked wryly to herself.

"Not yet," Et-chan responded nonchalantly. "He's worried about it looking like enjo kosai."

"Yeah, but he'd have to pay you for it to be enjo kosai, right? That's like prostitution, innit?"

"Like I said, he's clueless—he doesn't even realize!" Et-chan flashed a plucky smile. "He just keeps telling me to hurry up and grow up!"

"As if you can do anything about that!" the whole group exclaimed. Surely Et-chan's young man would be surprised to know the extent to which he was up for discussion.

"But has he ever tried to pressure you?"

"If he was that kind of guy, I'd break up with him."

*Ah, ouch.* Misa involuntarily clutched at her chest.

Et-chan kept on talking. "Of course I'm scared too. I love

my boyfriend, but I'm nervous about having to do something that I don't want to do. He knew that I was in high school when we first started dating, and he loves me too, so he'll wait until I graduate. And he knows I'm studying for exams this year."

Misa thought about her own boyfriend, with whom she was now wavering about whether to break up or stay together. *If that had been Katsuya and me . . .*

If she were to point out to Katsuya that he had misread kanji, he'd be pretty annoyed, and it would most likely lead to a fight (he was particularly sensitive about being told things he didn't know, always accompanied by a high risk of him becoming violent). And the two of them were the same age, so they had both been keen to go all the way, but if Misa had had any qualms, Katsuya probably would have fumed and accused her of not loving him.

Misa had never refused Katsuya, not for anything. She knew that if she did, he would get angry and hold it against her.

But had he ever given any thought to how she felt?

On the rare occasions when she had screwed up the courage to say that she didn't want to do something, had it ever occurred to him how hard it was for her to do that, or maybe to consider not doing something because she didn't like it?

*Love means not doing the thing that the other person dislikes.*

Despite the fact that, as a grown man, he didn't know how to use an iron or how to read the character for "silk" on the tag of his shirt and had to be told these things by his high-school-age girlfriend, Et-chan's boyfriend was still a good guy. He was a good boyfriend.

Even just from eavesdropping on this stranger's conversation that she happened to catch on the train, Misa could tell that they were a happy couple.

*I may be older than Et-chan, but I let myself be misled by Katsuya's looks and attitude. Turns out, Et-chan is a much better judge of character than I am.*

Misa was no longer wavering. She would break up with him.

This younger high school girl was much better at love than Misa.

But Misa was not so resigned to being unhappy that she didn't feel a twinge of envy, and she still had a sliver of pride left.

# Mondo Yakujin Station

Mondo Yakujin is the second-to-last stop on the Imazu Line and the station nearest to the eponymous temple. At the New Year, extra service is provided here, especially from New Year's Eve into New Year's Day, when trains operate continuously to shuttle the throngs of people paying their first visit of the year to pray for safety and prosperity. The locals refer to the talisman enshrined there as Yakujin-san, and though the area is urban, the temple sits on a small rise dotted with rice paddies that give the surrounding residential streets the rustic feel of an earlier era. Or so it had been described by a local classmate to Kei'ichi when he arrived here for university.

*Even so, despite how close it is to campus, I still haven't been there yet myself*, Kei'ichi mused to himself. His thoughts were then disrupted by the boisterous pack of high school girls that had boarded the same car. Older passengers were blatantly glaring in their direction, but Kei'ichi was the kind of person who, in such situations, could easily flip a switch in his brain. Still, every so often their coquettish voices pierced through the headphones he was wearing, so it wasn't as if he didn't understand their aggravation.

But, being a first-year university student, he wasn't so far removed from the experience of having fun and camaraderie with friends either.

Once the train glided into the platform, the number of passengers on this humble little commuter line would reach its peak—having accumulated six stations' worth already, it would take on one more station's travelers, quite the throng even on the weekend—before reaching the terminal station.

In trying to avoid the oncoming crush from the passengers boarding the train, a girl with a short haircut who had been leaning against the window on the opposite door collided with Kei'ichi, who was also standing there. She looked over her shoulder and ducked her head in an apologetic shrug, perhaps a bit apprehensive about his slightly punk appearance.

The title of the book sticking out of the tote bag on her shoulder was the same as the textbook that Kei'ichi had tucked under his arm. It was for a required course in the core curriculum, written by the professor himself and quite expensive. Students grumbled that he must be raking in the royalties by assigning his own book as compulsory for first-year students. A questionable practice, to say the least, and unscrupulous at worst, it had earned the professor the anger of most of the student body.

Kei'ichi assumed, from the sight of this infamous textbook, that she must be the same year as him, though it being a survey course, he didn't recall seeing her in class. She was neatly dressed in trousers, her look unassuming—especially when compared to the group of girls who were trying to stand out and reminded him of a flutter of butterflies.

## The Passengers on the Hankyu Line

Once the passengers had packed their way inside the car and there was a little more space in front of the door, she distanced herself somewhat from Kei'ichi. *Do I look that threatening?* he thought to himself, a bit offended, but then he saw her bend and crouch a little in order to peer out at the scenery.

*Is there something to see?* Kei'ichi wondered, already feeling a sort of affinity with her because they had the same textbook. He stooped his tall frame to peek out of the upper part of the window.

It made her turn toward him with surprise. No wonder—a sudden lanky movement above your head would give anyone a start.

This time it was Kei'ichi's turn to nod apologetically. "Uh, sorry. I wondered what you were looking at," he said. In response to her wary expression, he showed her the textbook under his arm.

No further explanation needed. Her guardedness instantly dissipated, replaced with a bashful smile. For the first time since acquiring the textbook, Kei'ichi was glad he'd shelled out the money for it.

In the crowded train carriage, she ceded some of the space between them as she pointed at the sky.

"I thought some kind of accident must have happened over there."

Her intonation had none of the local Kansai dialect that Kei'ichi had grown accustomed to hearing. He was from the countryside and wondered if she might be too. He thought he detected the trace of a Kyushu accent, while perhaps she could hear his own Chugoku inflection.

He looked in the direction that she had pointed, and off in the distance, in a blue sky that heralded the summer to come, he could see the dark shapes of five helicopters in formation.

"Ah, no—that's not what you think," he replied reflexively. "Those are Self-Defense Force utility helicopters. News media helicopters don't fly in such precise formation. See how, even at that altitude, they look like they're all flying along together smoothly on a single plank? And the intervals between them don't change either. There's an air base in Itami, so occasionally they fly over. I don't know if they're doing training drills or something else."

Kei'ichi suddenly realized that her gaze had grown round-eyed as she looked at him.

*Crap, I did it again*, he thought, jogging an unpleasant memory.

Back in high school, before he came up to the city for university, some girls had labeled him an army geek and made fun of him. He'd been in the school light music club, and the other members were reasonably popular with girls, but Kei'ichi alone was teased mercilessly. Occasionally a group of girls would ask him something about weapons or military stuff, and because he was so keen on these topics, he'd respond overearnestly, and then they'd laugh at him, saying, "He really is an army geek . . ."

Kei'ichi had been hurt when another member of the club told him, which was still painful for him to recall. "They even said, 'Too bad, because if he wasn't so into that stuff . . . ,'" which only made Kei'ichi feel worse.

He'd vowed that at university, he would conceal his military geekdom and reinvent himself, and now look what he'd done. He gnashed his teeth.

"That's amazing." The girl said this with what appeared to be genuine admiration, which Kei'ichi had a hard time accepting at face value, caught up as he was in past experiences.

"Sure. You probably think I'm an army geek."

"What's an army geek?"

He was disarmed by her sincerity.

"Uh . . . someone who's obsessed with military stuff and weapons? Kind of like a railway buff."

"Ah, I've heard about people who are into trains. Like, they know all kinds of things about train carriages, or what series train it is. They can recite timetables; they set themselves up on the platform with amazing cameras."

*I'm not into photography, I don't even own a telephoto lens*, he thought to himself, *but don't get me started on how they're actually called telelenses . . .*

"You can tell the different types of helicopters?"

"It's hard to know for sure, from this distance. I'd say those are most likely UH-1Js."

"Ah, but you can make a pretty good guess—it's impressive." As she spoke, she bent her knees and crouched again in an attempt to follow the formation as they disappeared behind the rows of houses. "What an incredible thing to get to see today!"

Her expression seemed so delighted that it served to defuse his somewhat cynical attitude.

"You really like those?"

Despite the fact that he knew they went to the same university and were in the same year, he could hardly believe that he was able to talk with this girl so easily.

"Well . . ." She gave her head a little tilt. The helicopters were no longer visible, so she turned to face Kei'ichi. "Doesn't it make you happy to discover something unusual or that you didn't know about? That's why, when I ride the train, I always position myself so that I can see outside. In particular, my favorite spot is by the door, where there's a big window."

That must have been why, when the crush of passengers had boarded the train at Mondo Yakujin, she had squeezed next to Kei'ichi instead of allowing herself to be swept further into the carriage. A person of small stature like her could get away with squishing to the side and still not be in the way of people getting on and off the train.

"I've only ever seen SDF helicopters on the news, so then to see them right here in the city! What's more, it's amazing how they're able to fly in such close alignment. This was definitely the big-ticket item of the day!"

"You know, we're the same year, we can speak informally," he offered. She had been sprinkling her words with formal keigo.

She responded automatically with a just-as-formal "yes," but then corrected herself with an awkwardly enunciated "yeah" and a nod. Perhaps she wasn't all that used to speaking casually with a guy.

"My name is Kei'ichi Kosaka. And you are?"

He meant it as an innocent icebreaker, but her expression instantly hardened. He had thought they were hitting it off, though maybe he'd gotten the wrong impression and she was simply a friendly person.

"Ah, sorry, I guess that was forward of me."

He offered a tentative apology, and she reached into her tote bag. From what appeared to be the inner pocket, she pulled out a card wallet.

It was packed with several cards, and from these she extracted her student ID, which she held out for him to see as she gazed at him with upturned eyes.

The name listed there read:

## MIHO GONDAWARA

He almost burst out in a laugh—without meaning any harm—but he quickly contained himself. Clearly this was a source of trauma for her. Like Kei'ichi being called an army geek.

". . . That's a pretty macho name. It sounds like it comes from the Warring States era or something."

He had barely managed to suppress the laughter that had welled up in his throat, but he wasn't sure whether the comment he eventually spluttered out was inappropriate or not.

"People have always made fun of it, ever since I was a kid. Even at university, I didn't stand a chance—the nickname 'Gon-chan' is just too irresistible. Whenever I introduce myself, out on a group date or something, people always laugh at me."

They may not have meant any harm (just as Kei'ichi hadn't), but that didn't mean it didn't still hurt, every single time. Even if she laughed along with them.

"When I got to college, I *so* wanted everyone to call me Miho-chan. But I screwed up my debut." She put away her ID as she said this.

Hoping to patch over this uncomfortable moment, Kei'ichi blurted out his own revelation.

"I also saw university as a chance to make another debut. All through high school, girls had called me 'army geek' and made fun of me. I thought if I could hide my interest, I might be able to get a girlfriend. But now here I go, unable to stop myself from blabbing about it."

"Oh, well, you don't have to worry—I won't tell anyone that you're an army geek." There was a slight hesitation in her speech, but she had taken up his offer to speak casually.

"When someone asks me about something I'm into, I get carried away and just jabber on—I guess I give myself away, I really am a geek!"

"With my problem, it's not really a matter of whether or not I give myself away . . ."

She pouted sulkily, and he thought, *Gon-chan is pretty cute*.

"The only way to change my name is to get married."

"Ah, you're right. I shouldn't talk about my problem as if it's on the same level as yours. Sorry."

"Oh, no, I wasn't trying to make you feel bad. I'm the one who's sorry."

There was a lull in the conversation until Kei'ichi broke their silence.

"So before you saw the helicopters, what did you come across today that was special?"

"Three borzois!" Gon-chan's response was immediate. "They were on their morning walk; I spotted them from the train on my way out. An elderly couple was walking all three of them."

He inferred that she must have had a lecture during Saturday's first period. He figured that wasn't a required course, it had to be an elective subject. It fitted with his reasonable assumption from her appearance that she was a serious student. In contrast to himself, who practically had to be strong-armed into taking just the one compulsory class during Saturday's second period (that of the aforementioned and infamous textbook author).

"Are borzois the dogs that are tall and really long and skinny?"

"That's right. One of them on their own has a lot of poise, but three of them together is something to see. An abundance of elegance, you might say!"

They were certainly posh dogs, and he imagined that the couple who owned them would have to be rich to afford the care and food for three of them, but to say so might have provoked scorn from Gon-chan, so he held his tongue.

He didn't want to throw cold water on her unguarded enthusiasm either.

"The Imazu Line is good, from here to Nishi-Kita, at least," she said. "One of these days I'd like to ride it all the way to the other end, at Takarazuka Station. But so far I haven't had a reason to go in the opposite direction."

"It's no good past Nishi-Kita?"

"That's not what I meant, not at all." Something curious about the Imazu Line is that it doesn't run directly all the way to Imazu; the tracks split at Nishinomiya-Kitaguchi. Passengers have to disembark there and cross over to a different platform in order to continue on to Imazu, two stations further, which was something Kei'ichi had never done.

She continued her explanation. "I'm living with my aunt near the Hanshin-Kokudo Station, which is convenient because it's close to the JR line, or if I go all the way to the terminus at Imazu, I can transfer to the Hanshin Main Line. Plus there are tons of stores there, you can get whatever you need. But the tracks are elevated after Nishi-Kita. It's much easier to spot interesting things when the train runs on the street level."

Kei'ichi had been nodding along as he listened. "Hey, you just slipped back to formal," he teased her. Her cheeks flushed as she quickly corrected herself, repeating the last thing she'd said but more casually.

"Go easy on me, please! Boys have mostly only ever teased me about my name. I'm not used to having normal conversations with them. Certainly not with a cool guy like you, Kosaka-kun."

*She thinks I'm cool . . . ?*

"Well, that's the first time anyone's ever said that about me. Like I said, all through middle and high school, I was known as 'army geek guy.' Meaning I've never had a girlfriend."

"So are you saying I have strange taste?"

"Hey now, don't go back on what you said just like that!"

"Ah, sorry, no! I've never had a boyfriend either!"

*She's funny. And she's cute. And we seem to get each other.*

At some point he had taken off his headphones, and they were hanging around his neck. Talking to Gon-chan was more interesting than listening to the same old music.

"Kosaka-kun, you don't seem like you're from Kansai. I'm from Nagasaki. What about you?"

It was the first personal question she had asked him. He took it as a sign that she was enjoying talking to him too.

"I'm from Hiroshima. I live a short bike ride from Nishi-Kita."

He may have overshared by including where he lived, but Gon-chan had mentioned the station that was nearest to her too.

"Huh, but isn't rent expensive in Nishi-Kita?"

"I got a late start on my apartment search. But I found a decent place that's only a ten-minute bike ride from the station, and the rent is pretty cheap. Actually, it's kind of close to the Mukogawa River."

The iron bridge over the Mukogawa River was the first one along the route from Nishinomiya-Kitaguchi toward Umeda. A lot of people who lived on either side of the river thought the Hankyu Line was a bit less convenient to get to, but for a student—especially one who grew up in a provincial city and whose primary means of transport was a bicycle—it was more than suitable.

"Oh, that's not far from where I am."

Based upon her response, he figured maybe the environment where she had grown up was similar.

"I can do my shopping near the station on the way home, and there's a supermarket close to my apartment too," he said.

"Oh, do you cook for yourself? I'm impressed."

"I don't have the budget to buy prepared meals or junk food all the time. So I crib from cooking magazines that I read in the store, because they usually have cheap and easy recipes. I make a lot of mistakes in the kitchen, though."

"Wow. I leave all the meals up to my aunt."

Just as they were speaking, the train had passed the last crossing before the station, so the impending pressure of disembarking passengers was gathering on either side.

As Kei'ichi subtly moved as if to protect Gon-chan from the onslaught and waited for the doors to open, he thought to himself, *I wish we could keep talking.*

At last they had reached Nishinomiya-Kitaguchi, the "terminal" station, though it isn't actually the last stop on the Imazu Line.

## Nishinomiya-Kitaguchi Station

Nishinomiya-Kitaguchi Station serves as a fairly large junction on the Hankyu Line.

The platforms for Sannomiya-bound trains (toward Kobe) and Umeda-bound trains (toward Osaka) are situated on the east–west axis; to the south of that is the platform for what's sometimes called the tail end of the Imazu Line. Add to that the platform on the north side for Takarazuka-bound trains, and altogether there are four platforms. Passengers ascend to a concourse on the upper level and then descend to whichever platform they need or, if Nishi-Kita is their final destination, they simply exit through the ticket gate.

Those who head toward Umeda can also get off at Juso Station, an even larger junction than Nishi-Kita. From there, they can continue as far as Kyoto or to any of the smaller localities in between that compose the greater metropolitan region.

All manner of people from every walk of life—solo passengers, friends, couples, families, work colleagues—traverse the concourse at a brisk pace.

But as they cross paths, the contents of each traveler's heart are a mystery known only to themselves.

∽

She wasn't in any particular rush, but when the train slid into the platform and the doors opened, Shoko was caught up in the surge of exiting passengers and deposited onto the platform.

As she was walking toward the stairs that led up to the upper concourse, someone barged into her sharply from behind.

Shoko was still wearing her party shoes with their thin heels, which made it more difficult for her to absorb the impact and keep her balance, and she tumbled to the ground. The bag containing the wedding favor had been dangling from her fingertips—that too was tossed to the ground, followed by the shattering sound of something breaking.

"What do you think you're doing?!" Shoko cried out before she even had a chance to get up.

A glum, middle-aged man in a suit called out in a shrill voice, "*Excuse* me," and raced off. He must have been in quite a hurry because, rather than come back to apologize, he pressed on, hurtling into various other passengers who showered him with boos and curses.

"Well, I *never!*"

The passengers flowed their way around her—not a single person stopped to help her to her feet. They stepped on her and even kicked her. *How could this be happening!* On the very day of her stolen fiancé's wedding! Just when her feelings had been soothed a little after stopping off at Obayashi Station.

Her fiancé may have been stolen, but perhaps she did have it coming, taking her revenge by crashing their wedding. Though it would have seemed more fitting had the thief and her fiancé himself been the ones knocked to the ground.

Shoko slowly got to her feet, confirming that she had banged her knee quite hard and there would be a bruise forming beneath the fabric of her trousers.

"Are you OK? That looked bad."

Shoko stood up. Someone was holding out the wedding favor bag to her. A group of high school girls were gathered around her, one of them holding the bag. These girls had been in the same car as Shoko, making enough of a ruckus to upset the public order and standards of decency, which had provoked the grown-ups to glare at them.

"That guy who shoved you sucks!" The girl stuck out her tongue in the direction of the man who had raced off.

Those fine grown-ups who had scowled at these girls hadn't bothered to say a word, but here were the girls themselves, checking on her and picking up the remnants of her wedding favor bag.

*Which of these two groups is the kinder one?* Shoko wondered with a bit of irony. She included herself in the group that found the girls noisy and annoying.

"It seems like whatever it was is broken." The girl holding out the paper favor bag shook the contents a little. "Should we tell someone who works in the station?"

"Thank you, but it's fine." Shoko smiled as she took back the bag. "What's inside isn't important enough. But I appreciate you picking it up for me."

There was hardly anyone left on the platform.

Shoko bobbed her head in thanks at each of the girls as they went on their way, then she leaned against a railing on the platform and inspected the contents of the bag.

A box, weighing more than might at first appear, wrapped with decorative noshi paper personalized with the bride's and groom's family names. Inside was a set of tumblers. The glasses featured a fanciful design that seemed fitting for that shrewd yet dreamy-eyed quiet type who had stolen her fiancé. They were tacky—not Shoko's taste at all.

When the groom had still been her fiancé, they used to laugh and make fun of wedding favors like these as they flipped through the catalog, wondering who on earth would ever pick out something like this. Clearly at some point he'd had a change of heart.

Four out of the five glasses in the set were broken. There was no point in bringing home a tacky gift that was mostly in pieces.

She took them all out of the box, wrapped each one with the paper that had been used to pack the glasses, and disposed of them in the station's glass recycling bin. She threw away the empty box and the bag in the regular trash bin.

At last, there was not a single remnant left over from that tainted wedding—from her stark white dress to their cheesy wedding favor, it was all gone now. She felt pleasantly refreshed, as if a weight had been lifted from her shoulders.

"Time to go home," Shoko said as she started walking along the deserted platform.

She would have expected her feet to be tired from wearing high heels all day, but her step felt lightened. Maybe it was her imagination, and even if it was, best to hurry home before her feet did start to ache. It was still a long way to Ibaraki, the town where she lived.

Shoko headed for the stairs up to the concourse.

༄

*Well then, if I've made up my mind to break up with him, better hurry up and do it.*

Having resolved her feelings of lingering attachment after eavesdropping on the chatter of Et-chan and her high school friends, there was no longer any hesitation in Misa's step.

Deftly weaving her way through the crowd, she headed toward the wide stairs that led up to the concourse.

Her boyfriend, Katsuya, had left her at Nigawa to go to the racetrack, but there probably weren't that many races left in the day, which meant that she didn't have much time.

She needed to retrieve her things from Katsuya's apartment before he got home.

Katsuya lived in Rokko, which was five stations away from Nishinomiya-Kitaguchi.

*To start with, there's my toiletry kit, the kitchenware I bought and some clothing. It won't all fit in my bag, so I'll stop at a supermarket and buy a big reusable shopping bag.*

Her thoughts were distracted by a commotion.

"Hey!"

"What're you doing, buddy?!"

Misa looked over her shoulder to catch sight of a glum salaryman plowing his way through the crowd, without any regard for the people he was barging into on both sides as he raced past.

It was only because she saw him first that she managed to safely avoid him.

*Wait a minute...* Just as Misa was about to climb the stairs, something else occurred to her. She turned around again to look for Et-chan and her friends.

Misa felt a lingering attachment to those girls, thanks to whose giddy girl-talk she was kicking her good-for-nothing boyfriend (as the old lady on the train had called him) to the curb, and she didn't want them to just disappear into the crowd.

The sound of boisterous squeals came up from behind her. And just like that, they had overtaken Misa and were gaily bounding up the stairs.

"How many scoops are you gonna get?"

"Definitely a triple scoop while it's half price! I'm getting Caramel Ribbon!"

"What about your diet?"

"I'll start tomorrow!"

Presumably they were talking about the ice cream shop that was located in the shopping arcade outside the station. *Half price, huh? Good to know*, Misa thought, but of course she'd be taking her chances if she stopped there today.

It would be a disaster if she were to run into Katsuya on his way home from the horse races.

"Et-chan, what are you gonna do for your boyfriend's birthday present?"

"I'll stop by Muji after we get our ice cream."

"What's your budget, then?"

"Three thousand yen!"

Three times what she spent on her father—and from the previously ruled-out Muji, no less.

Misa had recently seen a report on TV about statistics for how much allowance high school students received, and the most common amount was five thousand yen. Whatever Et-chan said about her clueless boyfriend, and whether she used that big a chunk of her allowance or had steadily saved up for his present, clearly she loved him.

*I want that too.*

At the top of the stairs, Misa watched as the girls turned toward the ticket gate and disappeared.

*Next time, I want that for me too, to find a boyfriend I can be myself with. And it would be nice not to be scared about him snapping if I tell him something he doesn't know.*

*Thanks, Et-chan.*

Misa headed down the stairs toward the platform for the trains bound for Kobe.

∽

On trains arriving at Nishinomiya-Kitaguchi, the doors on the right side (relative to the direction the train has been traveling) open first, followed by the doors opposite. The door on the left serves as the boarding point for passengers, so a line will have already formed.

Kei'ichi and Gon-chan were waiting for the left-side door to open, with the impending pressure of other passengers building behind them. It hadn't been their intention, but simply because they'd been standing by the window, by default they were now at the front of the line.

The doors opened and the passengers disembarked en masse. Jostled by the crowd, Kei'ichi found himself standing in a protective stance over Gon-chan.

"You said Hanshin-Kokudo is your stop, right?"

"Yes. And you get off here, don't you?"

Even as he nodded, it seemed a shame to say goodbye to her here. Kei'ichi had enjoyed talking with Gon-chan on the train—she was funny, and cute.

Though they went to the same university, their campus was vast and his chances of running into her again were bleak. At this point, all he knew was that they were taking the same required first-year lecture course, but he was also aware that, realistically, if he were to see her out with her friends, he wouldn't have the nerve to speak to her. He had to seize the moment.

"Miho-chan." Going for broke, he called out to her using the name she'd said she preferred. Sure enough, Gon-chan looked up, eyes wide with surprise. "Uh, it's just that's what you said you hoped everyone at university would call you by. Does that bother you?"

Gon-chan—*no, scrap that, Miho-chan*—shook her head vigorously from side to side.

Then she said, "Just that you caught me off guard. But I like it—even if it makes me feel a bit self-conscious. I wasn't expecting it, that's all."

It appeared complicated for her, but in any case, it didn't bother her. It had been worth gathering up his courage.

"Since your commuter pass allows you to get off here and get back on for Hanshin-Kokudo, how about it? If you have time, that is. I found something that's kind of bizarre near this station."

"I have time!"

Did Miho-chan take the bait out of curiosity or did she also want to put off saying goodbye? Kei'ichi hoped it was the latter.

*With any luck, we could end up at a café and hopefully I'll get her phone number*, he thought to himself, matching his stride to hers as they started walking down the platform.

"Look, over there."

Outside the ticket gate, there was a curved covered passage connecting the station to the shopping arcade, which stood directly opposite. Midway along the passageway, Kei'ichi stopped beside the handrail and pointed at the roof of a plain white building that was visible from that spot. Miho-chan leaned over the railing to see what he was pointing at.

"Wow!"

"Kind of unexpected, right?"

On the roof of what at first glance seemed like a nondescript building, there was a bright red torii gate, just like the ones that mark the entrance to a Shinto shrine.

"Huh . . . what's a torii doing up there? Do you think they built a garden or something on the roof?"

"But even if there's some sort of fence, you still can't see any plants or anything. If there was a garden, don't you think there'd be some greenery visible?"

"Well, maybe the owner of the building is a super religious person, or maybe the land it was on used to be a shrine, so when they bought it they moved the torii to the roof . . . ? Oh, I'd really like to know!" Miho-chan was utterly intrigued. Then she gazed up at Kei'ichi with a serious look. "I've got an idea! Maybe one day we can go investigate that building? It's super close!"

". . . You're bolder than I thought, Miho-chan."

Kei'ichi had been somewhat taken aback by her suggestion, and when he blurted this out, Miho-chan dropped her eyes, seeming a little embarrassed.

"I wouldn't dare to do it if I were on my own, but if you were there with me, Kosaka-kun, I think I'd have the nerve."

"Oh, you're counting on me?"

Miho-chan bowed her head, as if to apologize. But she persisted: "Though if you were willing, maybe we could do that sometime?"

Luckily, he found her persistence amusing.

"I'm not very relaxed with people I don't know, and don't have much courage, so the best I could offer is just to go along with you."

"Yeah, so long as someone is with me, I'd definitely be up for it. That's all I'm asking, that you come along."

"OK, so one day, then." He wondered if, when that day came, she'd really have the nerve to go through with it. "So, then, what would you say is the most special thing for today?"

Miho-chan leaned against the handrail to ponder.

"I don't know—the helicopters were amazing, but the torii is pretty cool too . . . hmm." She seemed vexed by the question. "I can't decide—today there might have to be two things."

"Well then, as a reward for upping your daily quota . . ."

Kei'ichi got a little tongue-tied. It was the first time he'd ever said anything like this to a girl. He willed himself not to choke.

"Would it be OK for us to exchange phone numbers?"

It was as if he could see Miho-chan's cheeks go up in flames. She raised her hands as if to hide them from view.

"Oh, I hate how self-conscious I am! I'm sorry, I'm not used to talking to guys. I know this is no big deal, but I get so nervous. Friends—we can just be friends. I know that's what you mean, right? Of course we can!"

*A little bit more . . . go for it . . . now is not the time to choke.*

"There's nothing wrong with being friends. But I might like to be more than friends instead."

This time Miho-chan froze.

"Uh . . . when you say 'more than friends' . . ."

"That would be my special thing for today."

"Er, but even on a group date, nobody's ever even asked for my number."

"I bet nobody can tell how clever you are on a group date. Because you're too nervous and you hardly say anything, right?" Kei'ichi spoke from experience. "Neither of us has any experience, so in that sense we're well matched, right? So we wouldn't be biting off more than we can chew either. It's clear from the start that neither of us knows a thing!"

Miho-chan, still red as an octopus, was muttering to herself under her breath, but then she bowed and said, "I'd like that very much."

Kei'ichi responded with, "It would be my pleasure." It was a very polite beginning—though to what, exactly, neither of them knew. "Maybe we can find somewhere to sit, so we can exchange numbers."

"Oh! I know a place!" Miho exclaimed. "There's a food court in the shopping arcade, and my aunt says that there's a stall where they sell delicious takoyaki."

Kei'ichi couldn't help but laugh out loud.

*Was it cannibalism for the octopus-red Miho-chan to eat takoyaki?*

"What—is that no good? There's self-service water too—so provided it isn't crowded, we can sit as long as we like."

That sounded like just the kind of detail a housewife might share, as opposed to a university student like Miho-chan—and yet he sensed that it was completely in character for her too.

"I've been meaning to try takoyaki, since it's a Kansai specialty . . . but, uh, that isn't very romantic for a first date, now, is it?"

"No, it's fine—I haven't tried takoyaki yet either since I came to Kansai."

Kei'ichi was already hoping that the experience of eating fried octopus with the octopus-red Miho-chan would be an unforgettable one.

The train departs from Takarazuka, taking on and letting off passengers before it arrives at Nishinomiya-Kitaguchi, where it will again welcome aboard a new cast of characters.

The rumble of the arriving train signals to passengers to hurry to the platform, and the ringing of the bell announces the train's impending departure as the last few stragglers make it on board just before the doors close.

Then the train slides away from the platform. As the Imazu Line reverses course from Nishinomiya-Kitaguchi to Takarazuka, what stories will its passengers carry with them? Only they can know for sure.

The train sets off on its finite journey, transporting as many stories as passengers.

AND THEN BACK AGAIN

*Bound for Takarazuka*

## Nishinomiya-Kitaguchi Station

The Imazu Line is a commuter rail, and so peak hours are—not surprisingly—the morning and evening rush to and from work and school.

In the morning, trains bound for Nishinomiya-Kitaguchi are jam-packed, and then from the afternoon into the evening, the crowded cars are those running in the opposite direction. On weekends, as the time comes for the last train, the throngs can rival those of the weekday morning rush.

That wasn't the case, though, on a Saturday after the university's second period had ended. Misa had just crossed over on the upper-level concourse from the Kobe Line platform and come down to the Imazu Line platform, bound for Takarazuka.

Perfect timing—a train had just arrived, so there were plenty of seats available. In these circumstances, you opted for the best and most comfortable place to sit. On an empty train, the majority of passengers were likely to select a seat on the end. These choice spots were available in the second car, so Misa settled in. She had been the first, but a steady stream of people continued to file in after her, and the bench seats were now filling in from each end.

Then came a voice.

"Itoh-san, Itoh-san, over here! There's still some seats left!"

Shrill and cringe-inducing, the woman calling out belonged to a group of older ladies wearing frilly and flamboyant dresses. Each one—there were four or five of them—was also bedecked in garish jewelry, and it being winter, they had on fake fur coats in a spectrum of colors. Their handbags were all designer brands, just the kind that female college students pined after.

Itoh-san had apparently still been wandering around in another car, looking for a seat, and upon being summoned so loudly, she arrived looking slightly startled. The lady who had called out was already occupying the seat across from Misa, along with the rest of her group.

*Uh-oh, I may regret taking this seat. They seem like trouble . . .*

As Misa was thinking this, a young woman was about to take the seat next to her. She was strikingly attractive, dressed with the sophisticated air of a professional.

But just as the woman bent to sit down, something unbelievable happened.

*"Hoy!"*

The same woman who had shouted for Itoh-san had launched her own handbag onto the seat next to Misa, right before the young woman sat down.

Both Misa and the woman stared in shock at the bag that had been flung onto the seat.

*What the hell just happened?!*

The older lady's companions chuckled, murmuring things like "You're too much!" and "Ugh, incredible!" But it didn't take long to realize that even amid their laughter and pretend disbelief, they didn't think anything was wrong with their friend's behavior, that it was an inside joke to them.

The designer handbag on the seat next to Misa had been tossed across the aisle in order to prevent the young woman from sitting there first and to save it for Itoh-san.

"Chop-chop! I snagged a seat for you!"

Itoh-san came scurrying from the carriage ahead. She too wore a frilly dress and carried a designer handbag, though her coat differed from the other ladies' in that it was a more discreet beige wool.

Misa opened her mouth, incensed enough to say something rude, but the woman from whom the seat had been stolen silenced her with a nonchalant wave of the hand.

"What a waste of a nice handbag," she whispered, even managing a smirk before Itoh-san arrived.

Unable to respond with an appropriately clever comeback, Misa nodded earnestly while the woman walked through to the next car.

Itoh-san seemed a bit quieter, compared to the others. She muttered an apology as she handed the bag back to its owner and settled herself beside Misa.

*You got it wrong. The person you ought to apologize to is the young lady who just walked away.* Misa's expression grew stern, so she pulled her textbook from her bag in an effort to take her mind elsewhere.

"No big deal." This, of all things, was the reply that came from the handbag-tosser.

*What a hag.* Misa could no longer contain herself as she sputtered under her breath. "Unbelievable. You old ladies are the worst."

She hadn't spoken loudly enough to reach those across the aisle, but it was likely Itoh-san heard her. Misa was spoiling for a fight. But Itoh-san merely glanced at her sideways, not saying a word.

The gaggle of older ladies seemed to be talking about the lunch they were on their way to, at a restaurant in Takarazuka. No doubt the place was expensive, and they must have been pretty well off to be able to afford such a lavish lunch on a Saturday.

*But I bet none of you have ever caught hell for the way you conduct yourself—not like what happened to me with that old man I'd never laid eyes on before.*

༄

Misa had been commuting on the train since she was in middle school.

On the way to school, the line she took was packed like sardines so there was never any hope of sitting down, but on the way home, there was sometimes the chance to get a seat with her friend Mayumi—depending upon the timing.

And by timing, that meant days when she wasn't on cleaning duty.

On those days, if she could make it to the station to catch the local train, she might just get a seat, but from the next train on, it would be filled with high school students who had boarded at the previous station, and there wouldn't be a chance.

In the beginning, whoever had cleaning duty would just give up hope, but at some point it dawned on Misa and Mayumi (they weren't sure whose idea it was) that whoever didn't have cleaning duty could get to the station beforehand and save two seats. Then, the one on duty would run to the station after the cleaning was finished, and they'd both be able to sit down.

It always came down to the wire for the one on cleaning duty, so they would get seats at the end of the car closest to the ticket gate. The one who got there first would save the desired seat, placing the other's bag there and sitting up very straight beside it, with one hand on the handles, every so often peering toward the ticket gate to make it obvious that she was waiting for someone.

How cheeky they must have looked. Even now, thinking back on it made Misa wince with shame.

"Whatcha doin' there, girlie?" An old man standing right in front of Misa spoke up all of a sudden.

Not realizing that "girlie" meant her, Misa kept up her show of waiting, still peering at the ticket gate.

"Girlie, there—you! The one letting yer bag take up a seat."

Misa realized he was talking to her, so she turned to look at him.

He was a balding old man, small in stature, but he gazed down at her with a forbidding look.

*Wait, what? This old dude's talking to me? What's he on about?*

The reflexive hostility unique to a person her age was easily quashed by his angry and unwavering glare.

"What makes you think you can take up someone else's seat when it's crowded like this?"

"Uh, um, this is my friend's bag, she'll be here any minute."

"That's yer excuse?! All these good people got on the train before yer friend there, but because you so guiltlessly saved her a seat, she can just show up and sit down?! You don't see anything wrong with that?!"

*How awkward—with you shouting so loud like that, everybody will be looking! It's embarrassing!* Misa cowered as she glanced around.

The looks that she had expected to be directed toward the disruptive senior citizen were instead staring daggers at her, the one who was still a child.

Though not such a child that these people didn't feel the same level of frustration with her as did the old man.

She was humiliated. Not because everyone was staring at her but for the reason that had drawn their attention. There were probably other students from her school in the car; maybe there were even some from her very own class.

"And . . . my friend, she'll be tired from doing cleaning duty," Misa offered feebly. She knew enough to feel embarrassed for using this as justification, but she couldn't help herself.

"In that case, ya oughta give her *yer* seat! That's no excuse!" Sure enough, he shut her down.

The fact that no one intervened served to put her in her place. And illustrated how presumptuous and cheeky everyone else found her and Mayumi's "brilliant idea" that they'd been putting into practice all this time.

"Sorry to keep you waiting! Thanks for saving my seat!"

Mayumi boarded the train, oblivious to the peculiar atmosphere in the car. The elderly man turned and pinned a sharp eye on Mayumi.

"So yer the friend?"

Confused, Mayumi inched toward Misa. "Hey, is this geezer bothering you?"

She may have meant to whisper this to Misa but it came out in her natural voice, loud enough for all to hear.

"Y'all've been up to this all along, haven'tcha?!" His bellow roared like thunder. "On a crowded train where everyone wants to sit down, but the pair of you think it's OK to let your bag save a seat for each other—who taught ya that?!"

Mayumi pouted. *Hey, you old geezer . . . what the hell?* Just as she was about to give it right back to him, he cut her off.

"Damn kids, what school do you go to? Tell me!"

*He's going to report us to school?!*

Misa leaped to her feet. "We're getting off." She thrust Mayumi's bag at her and bowed her head at the old man. "Excuse us. We won't ever do it again." Her tone was terse but apologetic.

By now Mayumi seemed to have registered everyone's disapproval of them. She followed Misa and bowed her head sulkily.

They fled the carriage and sat on a bench on the platform. The bell rang, signaling the train's departure, and the train pulled out of the station.

The seats that Misa had been saving remained empty, even after the train had left.

"For sure that old guy's gonna take the seat, once he's outta sight," Mayumi said, kicking the concrete. "He just wanted to sit there himself, that's why he had a go at you, for sure."

Both of them must have known that wasn't the case.

*Y'all've been up to this all along, haven'tcha?!*

They *had* been doing this, two or three times a week. How many passengers on those trains had been offended by their antics? It was demoralizing.

They'd been called out for what they'd thought was such a brilliant idea. By a stranger and in public, no less. Their behavior was conspicuous and shameful enough for the old man to finally snap and give them hell for it in front of everyone.

"He just wanted to sit there himself, for sure," Mayumi repeated, still sulking. Misa was sulking too. But they both knew the real reason for their funk.

Were either of them to break character, they'd burst into tears.

Obviously no one knew Misa's or Mayumi's names, but neither of them wanted to imagine how mortifying it would be if, say, there was an announcement during morning assembly that a complaint had been made to the school.

"Well, I guess we won't be doing *that* anymore," Misa said.

That was the extent of what remorse the two of them were capable of at the time—they didn't see themselves as being at fault, but the old man had kicked up such a fuss that it would stop them from ever doing it again.

The fragility of adolescence prevented them from being able to admit even the slightest error on their part. In a corner of their hearts, they must have felt a shred of guilt, because from that day on, they never rode in the first car of the train again. Nor did they ever use their bag to save a seat on public transport. What's more, they acted like they had always known that doing so was inappropriate and tactless.

Neither ever admitted it was the old man who had made them aware. But neither did they ever forget about it either.

∽

All of this explained why Misa found the behavior of the lady across from her so disgraceful, and why she sympathized with the young woman who had moved on to the next carriage.

*What a waste of a nice handbag*, the woman had whispered to Misa as she sashayed off.

The university Misa attended was mediocre, and her grades were nothing to write home about. Back when she'd been studying for her entrance exams, a friend who was a better student had helped her prepare, and Misa had passed by the skin of her teeth.

She would probably have to wait until she graduated and got a job in order to afford any one of the designer handbags the older ladies balanced so casually on their knees. And even then, only if she scrimped and saved and used her bonus.

For now, Misa took small pride in the fact that she would never act in such a way that she would be lumped in with the likes of the bag-tosser.

*Come to think of it, I owe a certain debt of gratitude to strangers.*
She shuddered to recall, but that had also been the case with

her ex-boyfriend Katsuya, whom she'd finally broken up with six months ago.

"*That good-for-nothing. Have you thought about getting rid of him? For all he puts you through.*"

On that day, they'd been on their way to look for a place to move in together, but he'd gotten into a huff about something trivial, and when she'd tried to apologize and smooth things over (even though now, she still didn't think she'd been in the wrong), he'd shaken her off and gone to the racetrack. He'd brushed her off with such force that she'd almost fallen down, and yet Katsuya hadn't even turned around; he'd just headed straight for the ticket gate.

She was sick and tired of it.

She'd become so used to being treated like that all the time, she'd stopped feeling sad about it.

*Disappointment. Despair. Futility.*

The elderly lady who just happened to be on the train had gently pointed out to Misa that those things were all that was left in her relationship with Katsuya.

She'd been right. He *was* a good-for-nothing, wasn't he? Misa had finally come to her senses and been able to admit it.

He'd started an argument with her over something trivial. That sort of thing used to happen all the time.

But despite his irritability and aggressive threats, kicking the train door in public was not typical behavior. Definitely not.

And although she had grown accustomed to his moodiness, she had no longer questioned him about it. That would have only stoked his anger.

But when people looked disapprovingly at Katsuya, she too became the object of their reproachful glances.

*He was a good-for-nothing.*

*Dodged that one.* She sighed to herself with relief.

But even their breakup had been filled with drama. He'd stalked her at home repeatedly. Had he been the one to break up with Misa, things might have been fine, but apparently Katsuya couldn't stand the idea that he'd been the one who got dumped (and by the likes of Misa, no less).

He'd show up late at night, ranting and raving at her front door, and Misa, concerned about her neighbors, would allow him in. And then he would hit her.

She would take the bare necessities with her and crash with various friends, avoiding her own apartment for days on end. This must have gone on for almost six months.

She hadn't wanted her family to find out what she was dealing with. She already lived on her own and hadn't wanted to cause them any more worry.

She'd even tried going to the police, but the male officer hadn't shown much concern. Misa had gone to the station on her way home from university, but when she gave him her address, the officer had brushed her off, saying she was under another precinct's jurisdiction.

He'd also told her there was nothing they could do without evidence. When she asked what kind of evidence, he'd said she needed a certificate from a doctor or something like that. Of course she hadn't had the wherewithal to go to the hospital for a medical report every time Katsuya had hit her.

She had, in fact, taken photos of the aftermath with her mobile phone, but Katsuya had found them and deleted them all—and hit her again. "Do that again, and next time'll be even worse."

Misa had thought she could take care of this herself, but in the end she turned to Mayumi's older brother for help. A strapping varsity guy, he was vice-captain of his university's karate team, and Misa had known him forever.

"Misa-chan is my beloved little sister's best friend." Katsuya had been summoned to a café in Umeda where the four of them were sitting—Mayumi's brother Kengo, Mayumi and Misa—with Katsuya basically cornered.

Misa sat the furthest from Katsuya, and Mayumi took it upon herself to glare at him scathingly. Kengo sat directly opposite Katsuya, projecting a calm, fierce smile.

"She's also like a sister to me. So I don't want you giving her a hard time—you get me?"

Katsuya was the type of guy who only punched down, so he was cowed by Kengo from the first move.

"I . . . I wasn't trying to give her a hard time . . . She's my girlfriend, and this is just another one of our fights."

"Misa-chan already told you she wants to break up with you. Isn't that right, Misa-chan?"

Misa nodded. "I want to break up. I'm done with him hitting me. And with him shouting and yelling in front of my apartment."

Kengo's arms had been crossed on the table, and he seemed to suddenly swell up even more in stature. Katsuya, sensing how Kengo was filling with rage, trembled visibly.

"So you'll leave her alone, right?" Kengo's tone made it clear that this wasn't a request. "If you have any objections, come see me on campus anytime. Stop by the karate dojo and ask for the vice-captain. Or I can give you my mobile number, if you like."

Katsuya shook his head, looking panicked.

"Well then, as proof that you're now broken up, why don't you delete Misa-chan's contact from your phone right here and now? You do the same, Misa-chan."

"Actually," Mayumi piped up, "it's better for Misa to block his calls from her phone. Nowadays nobody remembers what anyone's actual number is, so if he were to call her, she might accidentally answer without realizing it's him."

"If anything like that were to happen, I'd be there right away. But if it makes you feel safer, Misa . . ."

Katsuya, rendered practically speechless, proceeded to delete Misa's contact from his phone.

After they'd sent Katsuya on his way, Mayumi turned to Misa with a savage look. "How could you let things get to this point without saying anything?!"

"I'm so sorry! I didn't want you to worry, and you still live at home . . . I was afraid my parents might find out about it. And to call you—well, it's far away and so much trouble . . ."

"It's only Sayama! Anyway, it wouldn't matter how far, I'd come from anywhere! And don't forget that the giant demon god Daimajin lives in Osaka—you could've used him to ward off that jerk!"

"Hey, are you calling your beloved older brother a giant demon god? That's gonna cost you."

Mayumi blew a raspberry at her brother as she covered her forehead and swiveled away from him. "Don't overreact—does that really merit a forehead flick?"

"It's not as if my forehead flicks are lethal—get real!"

Misa was an only child and had always been jealous of their big brother–little sister fights. It had been a long time since she'd seen these two together, and the sight of them at it again made her well up with laughter.

And then with tears.

"I really have to thank you both so much for today. This has been such a mess, I don't know what I'd have done without your help."

Mayumi hugged her friend's shoulders. Her brother sipped his lukewarm tea with an uneasy expression.

Ever since then, Katsuya had abruptly stopped stalking Misa. That had been only a month ago.

Misa's phone was on silent mode, but she saw that she had a message. It was from Mayumi.

> Kengo has been worrying about you lately and wants to know if you're OK. Give him a call if you feel like it.

There was another text:

> Don't tell him I told you but last time he was home he said, "Misa-chan's gotten really pretty." He may be a Daimajin but he would never hit a woman, he's

the real deal. And all he ever does is karate so he doesn't have a girlfriend, you could snatch him up.

*I've gotten really pretty?*

When Misa imagined Kengo saying those words, in the same calm and confident voice that he had used with Katsuya, her heart skipped a beat.

But Misa couldn't bring herself to be the one to reach out, not having seen him for so long and then enlisting him to deal with the aftermath of her drama.

Then again—*Kengo had gotten pretty cute himself.*

He was a solid guy, relaxed and easy to talk to—nothing like that loser Katsuya.

Misa certainly wasn't going to do as Mayumi suggested and throw herself shamelessly at Kengo, but she could probably get away with sending him a little present as a token of gratitude for his help. Then maybe they could get together for tea or something?

And she did have his mobile number—when all that business was happening, he'd given it to her "just in case."

Before putting her phone away, Misa tapped out a response to Mayumi.

Thanks. I'll call him soon. Don't say anything to him, though, it's embarrassing.

"*That good-for-nothing. Have you thought about getting rid of him? For all he puts you through.*"

—*Yes, even breaking up with him put me through a lot. But I stayed true to myself, and I'm glad I did it. Thank you, ma'am.*

That's what she'd say, if she ever crossed paths again with that nice old lady.

And if she were to see that geezer who had scolded her when she was in junior high, she might even thank him too.

Oh, and Et-chan's gang as well, with their giddy girl-talk that she'd eavesdropped on. Even just thinking about them made Misa smile. She wondered how their studies for the entrance exams were coming along.

Misa made a wish that they'd all pass their exams with flying colors.

Thinking about these things made her forget all about those women with their designer handbags.

## Mondo Yakujin Station

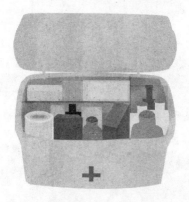

"Unbelievable. You old ladies are the worst."

These words were clearly aimed directly at her—well, at the group of women that she was a part of—and the passenger who muttered them was the young woman beside her, she herself not a run-of-the-mill good girl but a rather fashionably dressed collegiate type.

The kind of girl whose suitability she might question as a mother if her son were to bring her home to meet the family.

When a mother imagines the ideal girlfriend for her son—especially one he is considering marrying—she should be neither strikingly beautiful or flamboyant nor too homely as to be a black mark against her son's reputation. The ideal girlfriend is a nice young miss, the type who would appear neat and unobtrusively pretty, perhaps wearing a conservative blouse and pleated skirt. Of course, not the type who's overly bold or assertive.

At least, that's what her group of ladies thought. They all considered themselves refined housewives who enjoyed getting dressed up for a fancy outing together. That meant a satin or chiffon dress, accessorized with eye-catching jewelry and a designer handbag. All the more of a status symbol for having acquired it at a department store in Umeda.

Even buying it on sale, after jostling among other shoppers and snatching it away from another woman's hands—a department store purchase still earned top honors.

Then again, the housewives who actually *were* refined—the real deal, not wannabes like the ones in this group—could probably afford to visit the department store anytime, regardless of the sale season, to shop at their leisure and pay full price.

*Nevertheless* . . . Yasué Itoh stole a glance at the young college student sitting beside her.

Those who really were refined wouldn't dare to complain if their son brought home a showy girl like her who would say something as sassy as what she had just muttered.

Yasué had seen from afar the antics of the queenpin leader of her group. How she had tossed her handbag onto the seat just as that other woman was about to sit down. And Yasué had heard the crass burst of laughter.

*How embarrassing.*

She had been loath to join the group, wondering what the people around them would think of her.

But Yasué was definitely too timid to confront the woman who had thrown the bag. The way the queenpin saw it, she had done it as a kindness toward Yasué, giving her a leg up when she was lagging behind. Yasué was well aware of what might happen to her were she to defy that kindness, having witnessed others who had left or been ousted from their group.

There was nothing else to do but hand the carelessly tossed bag back to her. As Yasué muttered an apology, she felt an unpleasant prickling sensation in her stomach. She'd been experiencing more frequent stomach upsets recently. She didn't really have any interest in going all the way to Takarazuka today for an expensive lunch at a Chinese restaurant. Someone had gotten hold of their menu and, studying it, had remarked, "If we're going to go, we just have to try the fancy prix fixe," and so it was decided they would order the most expensive option, which was five thousand yen per person.

It being Saturday, her husband and son were home for the day, and before she left, Yasué had prepared fried rice for their lunch.

*I'd much rather go out with my family for such an elaborate meal*, she thought. Five thousand yen apiece! Now that her daughter had married and left home, that was more than the daily food budget for her three-person household.

Her association with this group had started back when they were in the PTA together for their children's junior high school. Yasué's husband and son, familiar with the group's challenging dynamics, hadn't said a word—they had always been sympathetic to her ambivalence about attending the group's outings.

When Yasué had handed the bag back and apologized, the queenpin had said, "No big deal," with an audible laugh. Yasué had smiled in an attempt to be agreeable. She had learned that the secret to getting along in life was not to go against the alpha.

That's when the comment, like a stab in the gut, had let loose from the seat beside her.

*Unbelievable. You old ladies are the worst.*

But what could Yasué say that would make the young woman

understand that she dared not refuse the seat saved for her by the queenpin?

*It's not as if I'm happy to be a member of this group,* Yasué thought. *I find them embarrassing myself.*

*Would you believe me if I said I'm ashamed to admit that you, young lady, tut-tutting, behave better than they do?*

*Thanks, but no thanks—next time, don't bother saving me a seat, I'd rather stand.*

The fact that Yasué lacked the nerve to say any of these things out loud meant being lumped in with these ladies and being among "the worst."

She envied those women who had long ago been put off by the group and whose names no one ever mentioned anymore. Having missed her chance to put them off herself, she wondered just how long her relationship with them would go on for.

"NEXT STOP, MONDO YAKUJIN. MONDO YAKUJIN."

Yasué became hyperaware of the absurdity of her husband and son eating fried rice that she had thrown together with whatever was on hand while she herself was en route to a fancy Chinese meal at a restaurant in Takarazuka.

Then she doubled over.

"Oh! . . . Are you all right, ma'am?"

The startled voice came from the female college student beside her. She immediately rubbed Yasué's back.

"Uh-oh, it's Itoh-san! What's the matter?!"

The group sitting in a row across the aisle appeared not to have noticed until the college student had called out. "Is she all right?!"

The women's voices rose in a chorus, but none of them got up from their seat.

"I'm sorry, my stomach's a little . . ."

"Oh, dear."

"Not when we're on our way to lunch."

"Are you all right? Do you really think you can go?"

Yasué took hold of the college student's sleeve, grasping it tightly. "Don't say a word."

The student responded in a whisper, "The last thing someone in a cold sweat needs is a lunch outing!"

Although it pained Yasué to raise her head, she strained to show the group a smiling face.

"I'm sorry but I'm afraid it's too much for me, so I'll get off here and go back home. I hope you all have a splendid time and that my absence won't put a damper on your fun."

"Are you sure? Well then . . ."

"Feel better!"

The train slid into the platform. When the doors opened, the student stood up to support Yasué.

"I beg your pardon. I'll be fine."

"This is my stop anyway, so I might as well."

Admittedly, Yasué would have had trouble walking on her own.

"Oh my, thank you, young lady, sorry for the trouble!"

The student made a show of tending to Yasué while completely ignoring the women who called out after them.

*Just let me sit on this bench for the moment. I'll fold myself up until I can scale this wall of pain.*

"Auntie, let me know when you're able to walk. I think there's a gynecologist's clinic just past the crossing. I'm pretty sure they do internal medicine too."

Her uncertainty made it clear to Yasué that this wasn't actually her usual stop.

"I'm sorry to have interrupted your trip and made you get off the train."

"Not at all."

The student sounded brusque. Yasué couldn't tell whether the irritation evident in her earlier comments—*unbelievable, the worst*—had dissipated.

"But I don't have my health insurance card with me today..."

"If you bring it to them later, you can get reimbursed."

"That would be a waste of a train fare to have to come back here again... and I always have stomach medicine with me."

"Well, you might have said so sooner." The female college student set off in a huff toward the ticket gate.

Yasué watched her for a moment and then opened her bag to retrieve the medicine. The bag she had bought with money she'd saved from her part-time job, though she had felt guilty about how much that sum could have helped their household budget—all for just one designer item.

The other wives in the group had pressed her that she should have bought more than one, or nagged her husband for another during his bonus season, but Yasué had demurred, saying that this one suited her just fine.

She took out a packet of medicine that she kept in her wallet. Her wallet was no particular brand—the other ladies had also remarked that she ought to get one that matched her bag, but Yasué had made up the excuse that this one had been a gift from her mother-in-law, so it would be a shame not to use it. The truth was that she had bought it at a discount for five thousand yen from the giant supermarket near her part-time job. The same price as the fancy Chinese set-course lunch that she'd been on her way to today.

As she was attempting to stand up to go and buy some water, the student had come back and was now handing her a bottle of mineral water. Apparently she hadn't left—she had just gone to fetch water from a kiosk.

"Oh dear, I'm sorry. How much do I owe you?"

"Don't worry about it, it's just a bottle of water."

Yasué bowed her head. She opened the bottle and poured the bitter medicine into it. For some reason, the student made no move to go anywhere.

"Um . . ." Yasué was tentative as she asked, "Why are you . . . ?"

"I feel guilty!" the student replied hotly. "I made that nasty remark so that you could hear it, and . . . if that's what caused your stomach pain, then I need to stay with you until you feel better."

*Oh, what a nice girl.* A very good girl. Even finer than the "ideal bride" for their sons that the ladies in the group talked about. This was the kind of girl she hoped her son would date. Those other wives might have their doubts, but Yasué would be proud to have a son who had the wisdom to bring home someone like this young woman.

"No, my dear." Yasué smiled as she waved away the student's fears. "It's not your fault at all."

Yasué would probably never see this young woman again. She could afford to speak freely for once.

"The truth is that I just had no desire to go out to eat at an expensive restaurant with those ladies. Especially not when I had left the fried rice that I threw together for my husband and son to microwave at home. How silly for me to go out on my own for a set-course lunch that costs five thousand yen. The thought of it is what made my stomach hurt all of a sudden."

Yasué paused before adding another excuse.

"Um . . . My friend who threw her bag onto the seat . . . she means well enough but she sees nothing wrong with doing something like that. Of course, I'm at fault for not saying anything, but saving a seat for me the way she did, it was really shameful and embarrassing."

The college student sat down next to Yasué.

". . . I'm sorry for making that nasty comment without knowing the circumstances."

"Not at all, my dear. As I said, I'm the one at fault for not having the nerve to say anything."

"I disagree, auntie." The woman looked Yasué intensely in the eyes. "If you had said something, the bag-tosser would have hated on you. If I'd known about the hating, I wouldn't have lumped you in with them. You say that she means well, but I don't think she really does."

"Uh . . . what do you mean by 'hated on'?" Yasué wasn't sure she'd heard her correctly.

"It's just a way to say she'd freeze you out of the group. It's a phrase we use these days."

"How interesting! I've never heard it before."

"So, you always carry stomach medicine with you?"

"Lately, this kind of sudden pain has been happening more often," Yasué replied softly.

"Like, whenever you go out with those ladies?"

Yasué nodded freely.

"'Scuse me for saying this, but," the student began, her tone not all that concerned, "what if you stopped being friends with those women? Before your stomach medicine stops working."

Yasué tilted her head as the student added, her tone a bit irritated now, "Stress is stress. Being in that group is clearly stressful for you, auntie, for it to trigger a sudden attack like that. But then once you're away from them, you seem perfectly fine."

Yasué herself had been vaguely aware of this, but to acknowledge that it was true would have only led to further troublesome realities that she preferred to avoid facing.

"Well . . . I've known them for a long time."

"OK, but let me tell you, auntie, those ladies take you for granted."

The young woman's words were so candid, and she spoke with such conviction. Yasué was unconsciously gripping the water bottle tightly. The truth was, she had vaguely known this too.

"When you're out with a friend who doesn't feel well, it'd be normal—even if just for show—to get off the train with them to make sure they're OK. That lot didn't even get up out of their seats. They were like, 'Oh dear, but we're on our way to lunch,' as if lunch were more important to them than you are. Auntie, it's like it doesn't matter to them whether you're there or not. Do you really think it's worth the effort of staying friends with people who take you for granted like that?"

"Hmm... I guess you're right." Yasué found herself nodding freely again. Especially in recent years, she had been enjoying herself markedly less and less whenever she was with the group. Maybe it was because once their children had graduated from junior high and gone on to different high schools, they were no longer bound together by the PTA, as it were. The only thing Yasué had ever had in common with those women was their children's school.

"Also"—and here the student's expression became stern—"better to cut ties with people whose values make you uncomfortable. Otherwise, the longer you stay with them, the more you risk forfeiting your own values for the sake of theirs."

*She must have had a painful experience herself.* Though she didn't seem to be all that much younger than Yasué's daughter, there was a note of gravity in the woman's voice.

"And forfeiting yourself might lead you to collapse from the stress. Look at how it's already affecting you!" She laughed out loud. "So what's it gonna be?"

Yasué responded with her own question.

"Why are you telling me all this?"

The student appeared taken aback. She pondered it for a moment and then replied, "There was a time when I was headed in the wrong direction and having a hard time, and someone I just happened to meet gave me some good advice. I just happened to meet you today, auntie. I guess that's why."

During the daytime, the Imazu Line runs in both directions at ten-minute intervals. Off in the distance, they could just hear the signal at the crossing, heralding the next train's arrival.

"Thank you. I hope you'll take the next train and continue on your way. As for me, I'll take the next train back home."

"OK. You seem better now, but please take care."

The student stood up from the bench and moved toward the waiting spot on the platform.

Just as the train slid into the platform, Yasué called out to her. "I will start by trying to put a little distance between myself and them!"

The young woman turned around to Yasué and, grinning, flashed her a thumbs-up. Once the train doors opened, she stepped inside without looking back again.

Which was appropriate for someone she just happened to meet.

As she exited through the ticket gate and headed for the opposite platform, Yasué was pondering.

She would start by increasing her hours at her part-time job. There was the matter of her husband's tax exemption for dependents, but she would consult with him and figure out the maximum she could still work.

Lately things had been tight with their household budget. And her son would soon be going off to university. If she were to gradually decrease the number of times she saw those women, then perhaps they'd eventually stop calling her—especially since, as the college student had said, they took Yasué for granted anyway.

If she were to mention her budget woes, those women might say that her husband didn't provide for her. He wasn't the kind of man to worry about such opinions, but Yasué would be much happier not to have to feel guilty about spending so much on a designer handbag just to keep up with them.

Instead, she would take that five thousand yen and her whole family could have dinner at her son's favorite restaurant.

And then, above all, she would be the kind of wife and mother about whom no stranger would ever say, *Unbelievable. Old ladies are the worst.*

# Koto'en Station

The squad of brash older ladies were so loud and unruly, Etsuko sought refuge in another car. There was no way she was ever going to retain the vocabulary she was studying on her flash cards, not with all that chattering and shrieking. They were as bad as a group of kindergartners on a school trip.

Now that it was exam season, Etsuko had already determined which university to set her sights on. She held on to the railing by the door with one hand and flipped through her flash cards with the other.

The next stop was Koto'en.

Etsuko's high school was in Koto'en, so she'd been commuting there all this time, but the university that was also served by that station was beyond her reach. Her first choice was a private university that had a respectable nursing program.

*I would have loved to go here . . . but it's just not in the cards for me.*

The station was always crowded with university students, each with their own distinct personal style. Vibrant and energetic, they seemed to be living their best lives.

Since Etsuko's grades hadn't been able to score her a recommendation for a competitive university, the guidance counselor had advised her to set her sights lower, especially if she wasn't going to sit for the exams at a safety choice. For this reason, Etsuko had decided to take the entrance exam for a nursing college, thinking that at least it would prepare her for a professional certification.

Her friends were each pursuing their own options, attending different cram schools. Now, even though they no longer had compulsory attendance at school during the week, they still met up there on Saturday afternoons under the pretext of a group study session.

It wasn't long until graduation. The bittersweetness of their impending farewell was what drew them to gather together in the classroom.

They called it a study session, but it was really more like a gabfest. Some girls had already been accepted at a college, while others still waiting to hear from their top choice were reliably sure they'd get in (Etsuko was in this latter group).

None of them were adventurous by nature. Though they may have appeared boisterous and happy-go-lucky, they all played it safe. Maybe they were just faint of heart. They weren't the type to really push themselves to reach for a better college, to assume the risk of failing and having to retake their exams next year. Instead, they opted for the sure thing.

Well aware of how precious the time they had left was, they looked forward to the chance to be together each week.

Etsuko—Et-chan, as her friends called her—was still with her boyfriend, the one who had a job but couldn't read kanji.

*The Passengers on the Hankyu Line*

"Still haven't dunnit?"

They may have been fainthearted, and still only superficially knowledgeable without much actual experience, but her friends never failed to ask Etsuko about her status. To which she always confidently replied, "Not yet!"

The fact that it had almost happened would be her secret.

∽

The teachers at both her high school and her cram school had told her that if she sweated it out until the end of March, she might just pass her exam. But they also told her she needed more than one backup.

She should set her sights lower, they said, especially if she wasn't going to sit for the exams at a safety college. But at the same time, she knew that they expected her both to take the backup college's exam and to keep pushing herself until the bitter end. As long as her backup was reliable enough, they advised, she could shoot for her first choice, and if that wasn't to be, she'd have Plan B to fall back on.

*Now is the crucial moment. Your future development depends on how you perform.*

Her homeroom teacher and her cram school teacher would egg her on with such slogans. It stood to reason—after all, it was her parents' money that would pay the fees, wasn't it?

To make use of the backup choice, assuming she passed their exam, her parents would need to pay the enrollment fee to hold her place. Even for a junior college, the fee was still a few hundred thousand yen, and if it happened to be a four-year college, the fee was closer to a million. But then if she were to get into her first choice—poof—they'd lose all of that money.

Etsuko was the eldest in her family; she had two younger brothers. Her family couldn't afford to spend so much on her entrance exams. The fact that her grades weren't good enough to get into one of the national and public universities put further strain on the household.

And yet both her teachers kept trying to persuade her to hedge her bets—they were remarkably insistent.

*It's not possible. My family doesn't have the money to gamble like that on my exams. I have my younger brothers to think about.*

Even if she'd left her cram school and found another one, she still had to contend with her high school.

Etsuko consulted with her parents and studied the exam schedules, taking into consideration the deadlines for submitting enrollment fees and prioritizing the institutions that would prepare her for a professional certification. All the while, her homeroom teacher remained tenacious as ever.

*Just think about it—you might get in there, and if you do, what a stroke of luck!*

*C'mon, give me a break already!* she had wanted to scream at him. "You might . . ." "Hedge your bets." "A stroke of luck." With those odds and knowing her family's circumstances, was he really telling her to gamble her parents' money?

*I wish I was smart enough to apply to that university. It's always been my dream one. If I thought I actually had a real chance of getting in, I might be willing to be selfish enough to nag my parents to let me take the exam.*

But even studying hard—diligently going to cram school—to still only be told that she "might" be accepted . . . ?

She couldn't ask her parents to hang their hopes on that "might," which, if she got in, meant throwing away the enrollment fee for her safety choice.

In other words, there was no way she could go to her dream university, even if she were accepted. Acknowledging the limits of her family's financial situation also meant that she was a grown-up now.

She would have preferred it if her teacher had told her that the university was beyond her reach. For him to have bluntly discouraged her. That would have been more compassionate.

*For me it wouldn't have been just a simple "stroke of luck"! Maybe for the school and for yourself, you see my stroke of luck as a boost to your success rate.*

Now, even just seeing her teacher's face made her feel sick to her stomach. His expectations for her performance hadn't panned out, and trying to avoid him was stressful.

It just wasn't going to happen—now that it was apparent, she would finally be free from all the pressure he'd been putting on her.

"So you weren't up to snuff after all." That's what he'd said.

*Did he have to be so cruel?*

Soon it would be Christmas. This was some present from Santa!

"You haven't been yourself lately."

Etsuko's boyfriend may not have known all his kanji, but he made up for his cluelessness by being kind.

Christmas Eve had fallen on a weekday, so they were celebrating a belated Christmas together on the following weekend.

When he had arrived to pick her up in his car, he had taken one look at her face and seemed to intuit that it was because of her exam studies.

"You're in the homestretch now. It's really tough. I feel for you."

*Wrong*—it wasn't that she was so worn down from all the studying. It was about her teacher saying that she wasn't up to snuff.

"If you don't feel like going out, it's all right. I can take you home."

For a moment she contemplated taking him up on his offer.

"Anytime you want to go home, just let me know. But first . . ."

They happened to be stopped at a red light, and her boyfriend pulled a plain white paper bag from his jacket pocket.

"I know we were going to pick out our Christmas presents together, but I wanted to give this to you first. I got it on my recent business trip to Kyushu."

The paper bag was printed with red letters—the name of the famous shrine Dazaifu Tenmangu. Inside was a pink omamori amulet for success in school entrance exams.

"I figured, since you're in exam hell, you need an amulet. I went to the shrine to pray for your success. I even got up onto the part of it that looks like a veranda."

"You mean the haiden, the hall of worship," she told him. "So . . . you think I'm going to pass my exams?" Etsuko asked, going straight to the heart of the matter.

"Well, of course! Why wouldn't I?! It goes without saying that I support you going to whichever school you decide on. How can you even ask?"

The light turned green and he started driving.

He got her a pink one for the simple reason that she was a girl. There must have been a bunch of colors to choose from, and he went with the pink amulet that now dangled in front of her.

"What do you want to do, go back home?"

"How come you're so keen to send me off?"

"I'm not! It's just with your exams, you must be tired. Maybe you don't feel like being dragged around."

"Yeah, but when I'm studying, I also need to take a break. Hey, feel like taking me to the place with a view?"

"What about your present? I thought we might go to Kobe."

"It'll be so crowded there today, let's save it for next time. I'd rather it just be the two of us."

When she said this, she saw his profile turn red.

"You're always so direct, but every so often you say something sweet. Why don't we head over to Mount Rokko?" he said, turning the steering wheel.

Etsuko had only just learned how grown-ups kiss. Previously she had always gotten scared and pulled away, but he had never pressured her, not once. She would hold back, unable to tell him that what scared her was actually how good it felt—and still, he just let her take her time.

No matter how many times they'd been up this mountain road, it always seemed new to her—this time he parked the car by the side of the road in a little-known spot where the view was indeed lovely. As they kissed, Etsuko always got nervous, her back stiffening, whenever a rare car passed them in the opposite direction.

Those oncoming cars had always coincided with her pulling away, until now . . . This time, when a car passed them, his lips murmured over hers with wonder, "You know, a car just went by . . ."

"Today, I'm OK with it. Kiss me again."

As if filling in the blank that Etsuko had requested, he kissed her with more passion.

She realized how much he'd been holding back all this time.

Their kiss lasted a long time, until—

"Sorry, I have to stop," he said.

Etsuko had been clinging to him, but he held her by the shoulders and away from him.

"Why?" She felt like she finally understood how to respond.

He sighed and leaned against the steering wheel.

"If we go any further, it'll be too much for me. I don't think I can hold back." He gave her a pained and embarrassed smile.

"It's OK." She wanted to give herself over to this feeling of being cherished.

He looked up at her, startled. Etsuko was facing straight ahead.

"Why don't we stop somewhere instead of going home? I'm ready."

"But—"

"I want to," she insisted.

Without another word, he started the car.

Etsuko didn't remember the name or location of the love hotel where he had brought her.

"I'm going to take a shower first," she said.

This wasn't a big deal. Nothing to be nervous about. There were definitely girls in her class who had done this already. Etsuko and her friends were just late bloomers.

She wanted to give herself to him. She knew that he would be gentle with her.

She emerged from the bathroom wrapped in a towel.

"What are you doing?"

"Uh, I just . . ." He was sitting cross-legged on the bed with his back facing the bathroom, his hands over his eyes like the "see no evil" monkey from the shrine at Nikko. "I have a favor to ask."

"What is it?"

"Get dressed."

Hearing his request, coming at this particular moment, Etsuko flipped out.

"What do you mean?! Look where we are! Are you not attracted to me?!"

"Don't be ridiculous, of course I'm attracted to you!" He couldn't help raising his voice, but his tone turned morose. "You don't seem like yourself today, you know. Maybe you're a little desperate or reckless. Haven't you noticed? You've just been going through the motions. It's discouraging, to be honest. I'm a man, but when I see the woman I love in such a miserable state like that, I can't just go along with it."

Shocked, she suddenly felt cold. He had seen right through her. He knew something was wrong.

For the first time in their relationship, she hadn't been completely forthcoming.

She tried to speak, but her voice trembled. She flopped down onto the floor and let out a childlike wail. "I just wanted to feel cherished . . . You went all the way to Fukuoka on your trip and you remembered my exams and you brought me an amulet from Dazaifu. I wanted to feel cherished by you. Today I realized for the first time that when we kiss, you're always holding back. So I wanted to give myself over to you."

"Ah . . . I can't . . ." He scratched his head audibly. "Etsuko, you're crying like a little girl. First you raise your voice at me and then you start sobbing. I give up."

*What do you mean, you give up?* she wanted to ask, but she couldn't find her voice. Her sobs had evolved into hiccups, but eventually he squeezed in a few words in between her sniffles.

"Etsuko, are you naked?"

"I have a . . . towel . . . wrapped around me."

"OK, listen. I'm at my wit's end. If this were to happen again, I don't think I'd be able to control myself." Then he turned toward Etsuko and held open his arms. "C'mere!"

She flew into his embrace. "Aw, crap, stop being silly," he murmured under his breath.

"I'm sorry," she whispered, clinging to him.

"Did something happen?"

While he held her tight, stroking her wet hair, she divulged the whole story that she had been keeping to herself all this time, which she hadn't been able to share with her parents or even her friends.

She also told him what her teacher had said to her—"So you weren't up to snuff after all."

*Tch . . . if he was gonna be like that in the end, then why'd he encourage me to try for a university I never had a chance at in the first place? I told him it was too much. I told him so all along! That I only wanted to take the exam where I knew I would get in.*

*I know my limits better than anyone.*

"Don't worry, it's OK. You're a good girl, a strong girl. You were thinking of your brothers, and of the burden on your parents, and about your future. Whatever you decide for yourself, Etsuko, that's going to be the right thing. Your teacher must be a terrible judge of character, for him not to see how good you are."

"You really think I'm a good person?"

"You'd be a better person if you put your clothes on. You're killing me, you know."

*All right.* She picked up her clothes and went back into the bathroom.

They spent the rest of the time they had in the room lying on the huge bed and talking.

She made a plea for him to take her on a trip, once she had started university and things had settled down. It could be somewhere nearby, she said, but she wanted them to stay at a classy hotel, so that could be her first time.

He laughed. "Now you're starting to sound like yourself again." Then he let out a deep sigh.

"But once you're at university, I'm afraid you'll kick me to the curb. A clueless idiot who can't even read the tag on his own shirt."

"Don't worry," she said. "I happen to love clueless idiots!" Then she dived at him.

"I don't get you, weirdo," he said, opening his arms.

∽

The train arrived at Koto'en.

As Etsuko alighted from the train, two college students who appeared to be a couple got on. The guy was tall and seemed kind of punk while the girl had a minimalist look, though she was pretty. She wore a necklace with a pale hand-blown glass pendant.

They probably went to the university that Etsuko had pined for. They looked to her like a happy couple.

But she wasn't jealous. Because her boyfriend was good to her and she knew how much he cherished her, even if he was clueless.

Etsuko headed for her school, where her friends were waiting for her.

# Nigawa Station

"See, look!"

After the train pulled away from Koto'en Station, Miho-chan—whom everyone except her boyfriend Kei'ichi called Gon-chan—pointed excitedly at the forty-five-degree slope that came almost right up to the railway cut.

"See the withered bracken? In summer it was chockablock with it."

She wasn't wrong. Like himself, Miho came from the countryside and knew how to identify such things, and those indeed were the unmistakable hunched and withered remnants of bracken on the slope.

"Yeah, that's definitely bracken. So?"

"Soon enough it'll be spring."

"Yeah . . . meaning what?"

"There are sure to be lots of fiddleheads growing. It's a secret spot nobody knows about."

He could tell where she was going with this but he pretended otherwise.

"And?"

"I thought I could go pick them."

There it was. Kei'ichi glared at Miho with a stern look.

"No way, that's a terrible idea."

"Why do you say that? They'll go to waste, untouched in the wild like that."

"No. Way," he repeated, pausing between words for emphasis. "Just how do you intend to get down there? It's along the railroad tracks, yeah? It's a steep slope, no?"

"Well, maybe we could tether a safety line at the top to lower me down."

"The railway cuts through the slope, and there's a construction site at the top. It's gated off, isn't it?"

"Maybe early in the morning, I could just slip past it. I wouldn't be going in there to do anything bad, just to pick bracken, and then I'd be on my way."

"No way."

"But the other day when I talked to one of the construction workers, he said they aren't doing anything with the bracken . . . He laughed and said if I could get to it, I could have it."

*Oh boy* . . . She was amiable enough—though in odd places and in odd ways—and old guys took a liking to her. Kei'ichi let out a sigh.

"I'm sure he was just joking with you because he knew there's no way you'd be able to get to it."

"I *can* get to it. I'm a country girl!"

"That makes no difference! What's gonna happen if you fall? You could really hurt yourself!"

"Whaaat? There are trees that I can grab on to, especially at that incline . . ."

"I'll be damned if 'that incline' isn't forty-five degrees!"

"Well then, I could go in from the track side, slip in just a little before the first train."

"That's an even more terrible idea!" Kei'ichi's eyes flashed with anger.

Miho pouted sullenly.

*Oh boy*, he thought again. She really looked pretty when she made that face. And he was head over heels. But no matter how pretty she was—or rather, because she was so pretty—he had to prevent her from doing this.

"Why are you so hung up on the bracken? It's not like it's anything special, as you and I both know."

"Because the pickings are right there for the taking . . ."

"But you could just go back home and pick as much as you like, can'tcha?"

Miho cast her eyes down and grabbed Kei'ichi's sleeve.

"If I go home for spring break, I won't get to see you."

*Damn, she's cute.* In spite of himself, Kei'ichi averted his gaze.

It just so happened that he had spoken to his parents on the phone the night before, and they had asked whether he planned to come home during spring break. Picturing Miho, he had demurred, using the excuse that he'd been back there for the New Year.

༄

Since they both knew from the start that neither of them had any experience with dating, it had the opposite effect of making their relationship feel more relaxed. Neither had to pretend that they knew what they were doing, and they were able to test things out together as they went along. The tempo of their relationship seemed to suit them both, since neither was trying to prove anything.

Even on their first date, eating takoyaki at the food court at the co-op at Nishinomiya-Kitaguchi, they had so much fun together and were smiling so widely, people might have thought they were punch-drunk.

Still, it wasn't until they'd been dating for several months that Miho started coming over to where Kei'ichi lived. She may have suspected an ulterior motive (which he might not have denied), and Miho didn't have the nerve to admit that she herself wanted to come over.

What finally got them past this stalemate was when Kei'ichi caught a cold.

She showed up at his place using the navigation on her phone to guide her to the address he had texted her.

"Kei'ichi-kun, you said that you cook for yourself, so I assumed you'd have kitchen utensils," she said as she arrived with ingredients to make okayu rice porridge, along with canned peaches. He had run out of rice so he was grateful to her for bringing over a two-kilo bag, but when he saw the book of recipes for food for the sick—for beginners, no less—it gave him pause. Especially when he saw all the pages marked with sticky notes.

After showing her in and then getting back into bed, Kei'ichi called out haltingly, "Um, you know, Miho-chan, my rice cooker has a setting for making okayu, if you like . . ."

He was worried about offending her pride, but Miho smiled

as she looked up while she considered which pot to use. "That's great to know," she said. "I thought it wouldn't do just to heat up a ready-made pouch, but when I practiced making okayu at my aunt's house, it wasn't all that great . . . I'm desperately hoping that the second time will come out better—it's kind of a do-or-die situation."

Her reply made him laugh, which led to a coughing fit.

He'd gladly try her do-or-die okayu—but on the other hand, he'd just as soon not have to eat something questionable. Even taking his fever into account, he was captivated by how pretty Miho was when she smiled. Maybe he wanted to be coddled a little.

She followed the rice cooker's manual and managed to make a passable okayu, and when she brought a bowl over to him, he asked her to feed him.

As usual, Miho's cheeks went up in flames.

But she obliged, tentatively spooning up porridge and blowing on it before bringing it to his lips. She also fed him the chilled peaches, using a fork to break the fruit into smaller bites.

"That was delicious, thank you."

"Thank your friend, Mr. Rice Cooker." With a bashful smile, she gestured at the machine as if she were making an introduction. "The next time this happens, though, I'll be the one doing the cooking . . . or at least I hope to be."

He welled up with laughter at the way she backed out in the middle of making this declaration, which led to another painful coughing fit.

"Quick, lie back down." Miho helped him get back under the covers and then asked if he had medicine.

"I still have some of what I bought." As he was speaking, he realized how close her face was to his.

... *Uh, is this about to be our first kiss?*

"I don't want to give you my cold," he warned her.

Miho said she wasn't worried.

"My exams are over for the semester, and I'm not going home until the festival ... so if I get sick, my aunt will take care of me. Plus, I'm pretty healthy."

As she enumerated her excuses, she brushed her soft lips tentatively against his chapped, feverish ones.

It was at Christmas when they took their relationship to another level.

Though they were both students with limited means, the plan was for them to have a little feast at Kei'ichi's apartment, complete with Christmas cake for two. They called it a feast, but Miho was still inexperienced with cooking and Kei'ichi's repertoire was limited to simple dishes. So the menu was a choice between temaki sushi or nabe, and they decided on nabe because it was nice to sit around the hot pot in winter.

They had already picked out their presents for each other: matching Swatches that they'd found at the Loft department store in Umeda. Kei'ichi had bought hers and Miho bought his. Still not entirely used to being a couple, they were a little embarrassed about going to the part of the store that sold his-and-hers rings and accessories.

On that Christmas day, neither of them had to worry about catching a cold, and they both probably expected that the evening would end with a kiss.

When the time came to exchange gifts, Kei'ichi handed her two packages.

"Wait, what's this for?"

"Well, the men's watch cost more. So this is to make up the difference."

"You didn't have to do that! I live with my aunt, so I have more flexibility . . ."

"Are you saying I'm to be pitied? I can't have that." His hometown accent had inadvertently crept into his voice. "C'mon, just open it."

They'd been dating for more than six months, so he had a pretty good idea of her taste. He was confident that she would like what he had chosen.

Inside was a necklace with a handblown glass pendant. The design was delicate, in pale pastels of mostly pink and green.

In the weeks before Christmas, Kei'ichi had saved up by working more hours at his part-time job, so this was within his budget, plus he had occasionally seen Miho wearing something similarly understated.

The saleswoman had also given him the hard sell, emphasizing how reasonably priced it was for such a unique item.

"Since it's glass, each one that the artisan makes will have subtle variations in color and shape. So you could say it's one of a kind."

His tone was slightly apologetic—the necklace had not been expensive—but all the same, Miho put it on right away.

"I love handblown glass! Thank you!"

Come to think of it, now he remembered that Kyushu, where she was from, was famous for its handblown glass.

"Ah, I forgot!" Miho said, clapping her hands together. "I have another one too! It's a Christmas present that my friends gave me today..."

She rummaged around in her bag, retrieving an oblong package that she held out with both hands.

"It's probably sweets of some sort. I thought we could have it with the cake." She began to unwrap the Christmas-themed paper—but then she suddenly became rigid, almost dramatically so.

"... Miho-chan, those aren't sweets."

The packaging featured cute childlike characters, but it was plain that the items inside were geared for adults. Miho was not so naïve that she didn't recognize what they were.

Miho's cheeks went up in flames. This time, even her hands, which had been unwrapping the package, were flushed.

"I guess I . . . was wrong . . ."

It was painfully clear that she hadn't known what was inside. Her agitation made him burst out laughing.

"Wha— I can't believe it! Why on earth would they have given this to me?!"

"Your friends probably wanted you to open it in front of them. They wanted to see your reaction!" Miho's friends could not have known that Kei'ichi would get to have the display all to himself to enjoy.

"What the hell were they thinking?! I can't bring something like this back to my aunt's house!"

Miho could just imagine her old friends making fun of her. *Why don't you leave them at your boyfriend's place?*

Kei'ichi suggested it himself. "Why not just leave them

here? Your aunt goes into your room sometimes, doesn't she? To clean it or something?"

Of course it would be terribly awkward if Miho's aunt happened to find these.

"But don't your friends come over here to hang out?"

"Guys wouldn't think anything of it . . . If you've got a girlfriend, it's totally normal to have them around. That packaging might be a little embarrassing . . . but it's no big deal—it's fine to keep them here."

From Miho's wide-eyed look, he realized that he'd said too much.

She raised her hand and asked quietly, "Do you . . . have some?"

It was a difficult question to answer truthfully.

"Oh . . . well . . . just in case. It's not as if I don't have those desires."

"Um, you mean, to use with me?"

"Don't make me mad!"

Her question had offended him. She apologized and gazed at him with upturned eyes. When used with the right person, it was the strongest weapon in any girl's arsenal—it made her invincible. And he was the right person.

"It's Christmas . . . we could take them out of that embarrassing package and put them to use . . ."

Having fired the shot that could not be put back into the chamber, Miho took off the necklace she had just put on, "just to be safe."

But neither of them had any experience with what came next.

He didn't want to hurt her or force himself on her—whenever she stiffened up, she'd apologize and say she was fine. But he could tell by the tension in her body that she was fibbing.

". . . Sorry, I don't know what I'm doing, so do you mind if I turn on the light?"

He thought it'd be easier if he could see if things were going all right, but she rejected his request with a yelp.

"I don't want you to . . . If we keep trying, I'm sure we'll get there."

Little by little, going by what didn't seem to hurt, they finally found their way, although by that time it was long past midnight and he didn't want to think about how many of the items from that embarrassing package they had wasted.

Miho fell asleep, whether from exhaustion or just from it being over, and as he looked at her sleeping face, he hated to wake her.

"Miho-chan, don't you need to go back home?"

He could not have predicted the confession that she revealed.

"It's OK . . . I said that I was staying out all night at a karaoke club with my friends." She opened her sleepy eyes. "I didn't know whether or not this would happen tonight, but even if we were just sleeping, I wanted to stay over at your place. I'm only rarely allowed to stay out, for special occasions."

"Just sleeping"—he wasn't sure that it ever would have worked out that way.

He wondered if she had concocted that story with her friends' help, which might have explained their present.

Kei'ichi got into bed too. After the night's desperate struggle, they would greet the morning together for the first time.

Apparently Miho had consulted with her friends about how to do it so that it wouldn't hurt as much, which led to them teasing Kei'ichi for a little while.

*Whatever it is, Miho-chan always wants to know the best way to do things, but I wish she would have thought about how awkward this is for me . . .* Then again, it seemed that the advice Miho's older and wiser friends had given her had helped, because she no longer grimaced during the act.

It turned out there was something to be said for finding the best way to do something.

༄

"OK, then." Kei'ichi nodded.

"Huh, really?" There was a pep in Miho's voice.

"That slope is too steep, it's still out of the question."

Even if she could figure out the best way to do it, this wasn't something he would ever go along with.

Her expression suddenly brightened when he said, "Instead, once spring comes around, we can do lots of hiking. You can forage for all the bracken and sansai, as many edible wild plants as you like. If we go deep into the mountains, I'm sure a couple of country kids like us can find them."

"Hooray!" Miho clapped her hands and whooped like a child.

*Is that really how college girls act nowadays?* This was something he wondered every so often, but that was also what he found so irresistible about her.

"If we get off at Nigawa, there's a trail at Mount Kabuto that supposedly takes about two hours. We could go check it out today? Even just walking on the dry riverbed, I bet we could find some wild rocambole and strawberry saxifrage."

"All right, let's go!" Miho paused and cocked her head. "But strawberry saxifrage, isn't that only used medicinally as a decoction . . . ?"

"Actually, I looked it up in a foraging field guide, and it said that the leaves are surprisingly delicious fried in tempura. It seems like there are lots of hiking trails along the Hankyu Line."

Miho stared at Kei'ichi, without blinking.

". . . What?"

"You went to the trouble of looking it up?"

It was a straightforward enough question, and all he could do was stammer in response. Miho had mentioned the bracken along the railway cut in between Koto'en and Nigawa a while ago, and though he rejected the idea, he had come up with an alternative plan.

He couldn't allow her to attempt the forty-five-degree slope alone, nor did he want to go along with her to do the thing that she had set her mind to. He suspected that the reason she wanted to pick bracken was because it was something she did with her family. Maybe she was feeling a little homesick.

"I just thought it would be fun too. I've got nothing against going to the mountains. That's why," he said, and Miho slipped her arm around his.

"Thank you. It makes me very happy that you would do that with me."

And now for the clincher.

"... So, the forty-five-degree slope is off-limits, right?"

He made her pinky-swear and then he changed the subject.

"So anyway, whatever happened with that torii gate? When we first started dating, didn't you say that you would get up the nerve to go and ask them about it?"

"Hmm . . . I think I might prefer to let that lie. I'm not sure I need to know."

When he asked her why, she laughed.

"Because that's how we met. My heart goes pitter-patter whenever I think of it, and I want to hold on to that feeling for as long as I can—and to keep the mystery."

Kei'ichi pursed his lips and glared at Miho, and then he flicked her forehead with his index finger.

"Ouch! What's that for?!"

Kei'ichi looked away as she put a hand to her forehead.

*Because you just casually said something that made me want to take you in my arms and hold you tight—but we're in public.*

The train stopped at Nigawa and they got off, Miho holding his hand while she rubbed her flicked forehead with the other hand.

# Obayashi Station

*O*bayashi *is a lovely station for a respite.*
    It had been about six months since Shoko had moved to the town of Obayashi, after the elderly woman she met on the train had recommended she stop there on the way home from her incursion.

Luckily, the company where she had been working had a fairly good reputation, so it hadn't been all that difficult for Shoko to find a new job. Whereas previously her office had been located on Midosuji Avenue in central Osaka, this time she decided to look for a job in Kobe. She now worked in sales for a boutique design firm in Sannomiya.

Her former colleagues had told her repeatedly that she shouldn't be the one to quit, but she had protested, claiming that it was too painful.

Putting on a brave face and smiling through it had been her final act of aggression. Her superiors had regretfully accepted her letter of resignation. Shoko didn't give a damn what happened with her ex-fiancé and the woman who had stolen him away.

Shoko's quitting meant that the two of them got their wish

and wouldn't have to see her anymore, and that her colleagues' sympathy for her and their memory of the scandal would fade as the proverbial seventy-five days passed.

It wasn't only the atmosphere of Obayashi that had appealed to Shoko—the neighborhood turned out to be very livable. It was the perfect halfway point between Umeda and Sannomiya, a thirty-minute trip to either Osaka or Kobe.

There were plenty of supermarkets and convenience stores, and her rent was quite reasonable. Shoko had told the real estate broker what she could afford to spend, and she ended up having too many options to choose from.

Ultimately, the broker found her a charming studio apartment that was a five-minute walk to the station, where the rent was even lower than what Shoko had originally proposed.

Her new workplace was rewarding. Or, perhaps more aptly, she seemed to have discovered that working in sales suited her.

Depending upon her workload, her weekend schedule was sometimes uncertain, but since she happened to be single at the moment and her friends were often busy, she didn't feel especially inconvenienced to not always have the entire weekend for herself.

Today, a Saturday, wasn't busy, so she only had to work a half day, and since she didn't have any particular agenda for the rest of the day, she had been on her way home. Perhaps she ought to have done a bit of shopping in Sannomiya; that way she would have avoided finding herself in the same train carriage as that gaggle of older ladies.

All the same, it was a first to have one of them throw her bag onto the seat just as Shoko was about to sit down. Any anger was overcome by shock. The young female college student sitting nearby appeared to have the same response. They were both stunned.

The female college student seemed to have a strong sense of justice, and was about to demonstrate it, but Shoko knew that it was more prudent to steer clear.

The bag-tosser among them seemed like the type to be spoiling for a pointless confrontation, all in the name of training for a group attack. Shoko could easily imagine it descending into an unseemly mudslinging match in front of everyone. She was loath to be drawn into such a scene, and she certainly wouldn't want to subject the female college student to something like that either.

Shoko had silenced her with a wave of her hand and the whispered comment, *What a waste of a nice handbag*, and the student, reading the situation, had reconsidered and composed herself.

Shoko had simply moved on, several cars further down, to stand near the door that, upon arriving at Obayashi Station, was positioned directly by the staircase.

She remained slightly concerned about whether, after she had left, the student might get into a squabble with the ladies. But as the landscape that rushed by shifted from "city" to "village," Shoko's worry receded. Beyond Koto'en, where the scenery became noticeably more serene, was her favorite part of the railway line.

"See, look! See the withered bracken?"

A couple who looked like students had boarded at Koto'en, and the girl—much shorter than the guy—said this excitedly as she pointed at the slope of the railway cut at the first crossing past the station.

"Yeah, that's definitely bracken. So?"

The tall guy, who had sort of a punk look, nodded. Something was at odds about their appearance—they didn't seem like they were from the Kansai area. Shoko concluded that they were pointing at the brownish hunched and withered ferns on the slope.

*Really? So those are bracken?*

Shoko, who had grown up in the city, had only ever registered bracken as something that might appear as part of an early course in a kaiseki meal. Similarly, when she ordered sansai soba with edible wild plants, she could never tell which was bracken and which was royal fern, or wasn't sure if those sliced vegetables with the hole in the middle were bamboo shoots or something else.

But these two could identify those withered plants as bracken, when they were out of season and quite different from what they looked like when cooked and served. Shoko eyed the couple with newfound respect.

The girl said that once spring came around, she wanted to go and pick the bracken, and the guy said absolutely not, no way should she try to get to a forty-five-degree slope like that . . . It was bittersweet for Shoko to listen in on their amusing exchange.

Bitter, because she envied their youth.

## The Passengers on the Hankyu Line

She missed what happened next in their discussion to merit the guy suddenly flicking his girl's forehead. The girl might have protested, but from an outsider's perspective, it was clear what was going on.

When the boyfriend had looked away from her, his cheeks were such a deep shade of vermilion, it looked as if the color had been painted on with a brush. His girlfriend must have said something especially endearing to him. He was so much taller that, by huddling close to her, she wouldn't be able to see the color of his cheeks—he was using his height to hide his embarrassment—though when they got off at Nigawa, she still seemed a little unhappy.

After they disembarked, the train sped on toward Obayashi. Shoko had never actually timed it, but she had the sense that the interval between Nigawa and Obayashi was the longest distance between stops along the Imazu Line. The landscape became more and more mountainous, and to Shoko, who had only ever lived in urban environments, their vividness was still a novelty. Despite what it may have felt like, the train line was rather compact—on a bicycle, from Obayashi to Nigawa was only about a ten-minute ride, and probably not even half an hour to get to Nishinomiya-Kitaguchi.

Before reaching Obayashi Station, the train pitched sharply. Maybe the driver was a rookie, because the braking wasn't smooth at all, and Shoko, caught off guard, had to hastily grab on to a strap to keep her balance.

But she had estimated perfectly, and in the station, the door opened right in front of the staircase. As Shoko stepped off the train, a chorus of high-pitched screams came rushing down the stairs.

It was a group of girls wearing yellow caps and red randoseru backpacks, probably in their first or second year of elementary school.

It had seemed like they were rushing to catch the train, but there was something else going on. They darted behind the staircase, toward the rear of the train where there was an escalator, and stood there snickering.

Despite their young age, there was already a girlish spitefulness in the way they laughed, and Shoko knitted her brows together.

Unaware that there was an adult on the other side of the staircase observing and listening to their antics, the girls started talking conspiratorially. Their voices were fairly loud for telling secrets, probably because of their excitement.

"OK, A-chan, you hide here! Then when B-san comes along, we'll pretend not to know where you are and we'll make her leave!"

"Uh, OK . . ." The one being made to hide, presumably A-chan, sounded confused.

Shoko sensed someone coming and looked up to see that a girl had stopped midway down the stairs. She too had on a yellow cap and a red randoseru backpack. This must have been B-san.

B-san had a sort of tense look on her face as she came down the rest of the stairs. She passed by Shoko and headed toward the other girls.

Shoko leaned casually against the stairs' handrail, curious to see how this would play out.

"Oh, B-san!" exclaimed the girl who seemed to be the leader of the pack, her voice sweet and fake. "If you're looking for A-chan, I think she left without you! We were looking for her too—she must have taken the earlier train?"

B-san hadn't asked them anything about A-chan. Keeping a wary distance from the group, she stood there, on edge, completely ignoring the girl who was putting on the show and the others behind her who were unable to hold back their snickers.

A-chan was still hiding behind the staircase, only a few steps away.

As B-san stood rooted to the spot, the leader of the group suddenly playacted concern.

"Didn't you hear? I said, A-chan already went home!"

Shoko was behind B-san and couldn't tell what her expression was.

"Thank you for telling me, even though I didn't ask."

*Well said!* Shoko thought.

As B-san again passed alongside Shoko, who was now inadvertently fully absorbed in this drama, the girl's expression remained tense, though she showed no sign of tears. She kept walking toward the front of the platform, all the way to the end, where she took a seat on the bench that was the furthest away.

Her erect posture conveyed a specific message:

*Fine. I won't look over there, even when the next train arrives. And don't worry, once we're on the train, I won't check to see whether or not A-chan is with you either.*

As young as they were, these girls were already like women. Spiteful, indecisive and prideful. Quite a range of femininity was already on display in this little circle.

Something about B-san's young pridefulness was compelling to Shoko. She walked over to where B-san sat on the bench.

"Mind if I sit next to you?"

B-san looked up at Shoko dubiously. The self-assertive set of her features reminded Shoko of her younger self.

". . . Go ahead."

Nowadays children probably received strict instructions not to talk to strangers. It was perfectly clear that B-san was skeptical of Shoko.

"You don't know me at all, but don't worry, I mean you no harm."

". . . OK."

"I just wanted to tell you how much I admired the way you handled those girls back there."

B-san's eyes grew wide, and then her tears seemed to spill over uncontrollably.

Shoko took a handkerchief out of her bag and handed it to her. She'd read that recently, for security purposes, elementary school students no longer wore name tags. If she hadn't overheard the girls' loud whispering earlier, she wouldn't have been able to guess her name.

"Here, take this, you can have it."

"But my mom will get mad at me . . ."

"You can tell her that you fell down and a nice lady gave it to you. When the train comes, you don't want them to know you've been crying. For now, they can't see past me."

B-san pursed her lips tightly and, without speaking, began to wipe her eyes with the handkerchief. So proud.

Shoko peeked over her shoulder and could tell that the girls in the group excluding B-san were trying to figure out what was going on here.

"For a girl like you, life might not be all that easy. But that doesn't mean that you won't find people who see you. There will be plenty of people who admire the way you handle yourself. Like I do."

*So keep your chin up.*

B-san looked up from behind the handkerchief.

"Are *you* happy?"

The girl's question prodded a tender spot for Shoko. She forced a smile and offered the following:

"I thought I was on the way to being happy, but I had a little setback and I'm in the midst of starting over."

*My new job is going well. I moved to a wonderful new place. And—when happiness betrayed me, I took my revenge. I have no regrets.*

"But I don't regret it. I'm getting a bit of a later start, but I still believe I'll find happiness."

"Then I believe I can find it too!"

They heard the distant clanging of the bell at the crossing. The next train about to arrive was bound for Nishinomiya-Kitaguchi.

The train came and went on the opposite platform, and then there was the sound of the bell at the crossing for the train that would arrive on this platform.

"Well then, take care of yourself."

Shoko stood up, and the girl smiled and waved at her. She sat up even taller and looked straight in front of her. So as not to see her enemies.

When she got to the staircase, Shoko paused. She regarded the girls coldly. They were still children, and yet already women. They did not merit any indulgence. The girls could already sense scorn in the way that Shoko looked at them. But instead of returning her gaze, all they could do was avert their eyes awkwardly.

Even at their age, girls will assess their rivals' rank and treat them accordingly, and Shoko knew enough not to allow herself to be taken in by children. She was capable of intimidating almost anyone, be they young or old, man or woman. She was good at hiding her fangs, but then once her fangs had been bared, she knew how to go in for the kill.

That elderly woman she'd never met before had expressed her concern, or rather her remonstrance:

*It can be hard for a woman like you to find happiness.*

Shoko forced a smile as she thought about B-san and her pride.

They had made a pact together, to each find happiness. Like what that young couple who had gotten off at Nigawa seemed to have with each other. Happiness that meant not being triggered by the sight of new love.

Shoko was halfway up the stairs when the train slid into the platform. As the doors opened and passengers poured out—

"You there . . . !"

Among the commotion of disembarking passengers, a voice

rang out and then the clack of heels bounding up the stairs. Shoko realized that the voice and the footsteps were directed toward her, so she turned around.

"It *is* you! We saw each other before."

It was the female college student she had encountered on the train, when the designer bag had been thrown onto the seat.

"What are you doing here? Weren't you on the previous train?"

"I could say the same to you—what brings you here now, on the later train? I certainly hope there wasn't a row with those ladies . . . ?"

"Oh, no, nothing like that." The student waved her hand in front of her face to ease Shoko's concern. "Just experiencing life's rich pageant."

Shoko chuckled at her odd choice of words.

"As a matter of fact, I myself had a taste of life's rich pageant right after I got off the train."

As they walked side by side along the passage heading toward the west ticket gate, the student was the one to chuckle.

"But who'da thought it—quite an amazing coincidence!"

"Truly!"

Shoko felt almost cheerful. Maybe a seed of happiness had been tossed her way.

"Say, if you have the time, would you like to get a coffee? My taste of life's rich pageant is worth sharing."

"I'd love to! I can tell you about my pageant too."

"Does it have anything to do with me?"

"It does! I mean, you were there, so . . ."

*Hmm, could it have to do with that gaggle of ladies?* Shoko's curiosity was piqued.

"I only just recently moved here, so I don't know the area very well. Do you know a place?"

"Do you mind going over to Koma Road? There's an Italian restaurant where you can order a cake special that comes with coffee—and the refills are free."

"Koma Road, you say?"

"It goes toward Nakatsuhama."

"Ah, I think I've heard of it—if you turn right at the intersection where the wholesale supermarket is—is that where you mean?"

"Yes, that's right. It's inexpensive and it's pretty good too."

The student's suggestion was probably made with her own limited budget in mind. Shoko could have easily treated her, no matter how fancy the place, but that wasn't what this was about. She had a feeling that despite the difference in their ages, the two of them could be friends. But if Shoko were to pay the first time, it would set them up on an unequal footing, and then their connection might not have a chance to develop. That's why it was better to go along with the reasonably priced option.

"It might not be ritzy enough for you, though . . ."

*See, she's already feeling inferior!*

"Not at all. I may have a job, but I live on my own and have to economize. Sometimes it's worth indulging yourself, but I love a good bargain—like the discounts at the supermarket right before the store's about to close, or a conveyor-belt sushi restaurant!"

"In that case, let's go!"

To the outside eye, they might have looked like sisters. The thought made Shoko smile.

There it was, her first step toward happiness.

And after this cake-and-coffee date, she will have made a new friend. Which, at her age, was not such an easy thing to do.

# Sakasegawa Station

*My heavens.*

Tokié gazed casually at the young couple who stood waiting at the next boarding spot on the platform for the train bound for Takarazuka.

As one aged, the days seemed to fly by. A year passed without her even realizing it, and what happened six months ago felt like it was just yesterday.

Tokié immediately recalled having seen that enormous canvas tote bag, brightly printed with a certain internationally recognizable mouse.

Back then, the young woman carrying it had been on the opposite platform, midway along the stairs. And the young man standing next to her now had been trying earnestly to persuade her to accept an invitation somewhere, while she smiled back at him.

That heartwarming scene of budding romance that Tokié had just happened to witness appeared to have developed into a full-fledged relationship. The two of them stood there now, hands lightly interlaced, talking and laughing as they waited for the train.

Tokié herself was waiting for the train with her granddaughter Ami and holding the carrier for her miniature dachshund. Ami had wanted to name the dog something vaguely genteel and French-sounding like Marron or Chocolat, but naming rights were under the authority of the pet's owner.

Tokié would have preferred to get a Japanese dog breed, but not many of them were small enough. She'd learned that a Shiba Inu, for instance, required a significant amount of daily exercise, and thus might not be the best breed for someone her age.

There was also a miniature version called the Mame Shiba Inu, but Tokié had heard that some so-called mini Shiba Inu still grew to be the same size as a regular Shiba Inu, and that was a risk she wasn't willing to take.

In the end, Tokié went with a breed that Ami had wanted, a black long-haired miniature dachshund, though she would not budge on the dog's name.

Ken was his name. It was the same as the Kai Ken that Tokié's parents had long ago, who had lived until around the time when Tokié's son had started nursery school. Her son seemed not to remember this detail—he had made the comment about the fact that since "*ken*" was one way to read the kanji for "dog," it wasn't a very ingenious name.

Ami, for her part, was upset that Tokié hadn't chosen a more charming name, but Tokié was unmoved. She was certainly not the type of grandmother who would go to such lengths to indulge her granddaughter.

After about half a year had passed, though, Ami seemed to have come around to the name Ken. And the dog was fulfilling its purpose: Ami started staying over at Tokié's house; in fact, the night before, her daughter-in-law had brought Ami over on the way home from nursery school, apologizing and asking whether Tokié minded taking care of her. Ever since she had gotten Ken, it seemed that Tokié's home had been transformed into a de facto overnight play school.

"Granny, let me hold Ken's carrier!"

"No, dear. You asked before and you wouldn't have made it all the way down the staircase just now, would you?"

"I can hold it just fine while we're waiting!"

Not wanting Ami to make any more of a fuss before the train arrived, Tokié relented and handed the carrier to Ami.

"Step back a little. You mustn't drop the carrier. If it even looks like you aren't holding it properly, I'll make you give it right back to me."

As expected, Ami wasn't able to hold on to it for the duration of their wait.

"Here, I'm giving it back," she said.

"What did I tell you?"

Just as Tokié took the carrier back from Ami, they heard the signal at the crossing for the oncoming train.

As it turned out, there was absolutely no reason for Tokié to have been concerned about whether Ami would make a fuss before they got on the train.

*Never in my life have I been on a train that was so unruly!*

The moment the train doors opened, shrill female voices gushed forth, chattering and laughing. Had these belonged to young children or students, Tokié might have been willing to look the other way without giving much further thought, but in this case she couldn't help wondering why, when women reach a certain age, they appeared to lose all sense of decency.

The train car seemed so full of their frisky cries, at first Tokié thought the ladies had taken over half of the seats, but in reality they only numbered five or six—their chitter-chatter was just that loud. It didn't help that despite the fact that they were sitting in a row along one bench, they were trying to have a single conversation together, so they were all shouting at the top of their lungs.

It was no coincidence that there were only a few other passengers sharing this car with them. Those who were riding with them appeared impatient or didn't try to hide their annoyance, but the housewives kept babbling on, seemingly oblivious.

The din was such that when Tokié boarded the train, Ken whimpered through his nose, perhaps out of fear. One of the housewives actually seemed to notice, because she looked over at the carrier Tokié was holding and made a little frown.

The door through which they had boarded left them as close as possible to where the ladies were sitting, and Tokié wanted to put some distance between them if possible. She took Ami by the hand and stood near the opposite door.

Ami was staring with keen interest at these ladies squawking like tropical birds. It couldn't be helped—young children were attracted by sound and light. And the women were so raucous that even the grown-ups found it painful to ignore them.

Ami was at that vexing age when she insisted on asking why or how come certain things were the way they were.

"Granny"—she looked up at Tokié and then turned toward

the housewives—"how come they're making so much noise, even though they're grown-ups?"

Worried that Tokié might not be able to hear her over the women's talking, Ami had raised her own voice to pose her innocent question, making it audible to more people than she might have intended, and several of the other passengers let out a suppressed giggle.

"When we went on a field trip at nursery school, our teacher told us to be quiet on the train. But for grown-ups, it's OK?"

Again, there were a few giggles.

Tokié looked down at her granddaughter and shrugged. *I see that you too like to point out when things don't make sense. I wonder where you get that from?*

There was a pause in the housewives' chatter as they looked over and glared, with brows arched.

"Hey! What are you teaching that child?"

The one who lit the spark was sitting in the middle of the group, the apparent queenpin.

Now Tokié herself spun around to face them.

"I am teaching my granddaughter the basic rules of civility."

Tokié's sharp retort elicited further sneers from other passengers, and the housewives' faces flushed with anger.

"Wha . . . What do you mean by 'civility' when you're the one bringing a dog onto the train?! If that's what you think is civilized, then it's easy to imagine what's in store for that child!"

*Well, I'll be. Look who's picking a fight.*

*What's in store for this child is a matter of my son and his wife's concern—and my own.*

Holding Ken's carrier in one hand and taking Ami's hand with the other, Tokié briskly walked over to stand in front of the housewives.

Her assured step belied her age, and the women seemed to quaver ever so slightly. They must not have expected her to step right up to the challenge.

"Hear now." Tokié began speaking in a firm tone, like the one she used when she taught high school. "Provided that one pays the designated fare, one may rightfully bring a dog or a cat that is in a carrier onto the train. My granddaughter and I are in compliance with the rules of bringing a pet onto the train. Here is our ticket."

Tokié took Ken's pet-fare ticket out from her purse and held it up to show the women.

"Your remarks that we are lacking in civility have no basis in fact. We are abiding by the rules and regulations of Hankyu Railway, so if you have any objections, bring those up with the railway company."

The comeback came from another direction.

"It stinks!" cried the woman who had frowned at Tokié and Ami when they got on the train with the carrier. Rather than meet Tokié's gaze, she locked eyes with Ami. "That dog stinks! I can't stand the smell, so keep away from me!"

Ami's face turned bright red.

"He does not! I gave Ken a shampoo myself just yesterday! I bathe him regularly, so he definitely does not stink!"

"How can you even tell what the dog smells like?" the voice of a young woman chimed in.

Without anyone noticing, that heartwarming couple had

entered the fray. The voice belonged to the young woman carrying the canvas tote bag with the internationally recognized mouse on it.

"The air in here reeks of so much perfume it makes me sneeze."

"It's nauseating, isn't it?" Her boyfriend nodded in agreement.

The fresh young beauty flashed a smile at the band of housewives.

"It seems you're wearing quite expensive perfume, but perhaps you don't know the proper way to apply it? Just a dab behind the ears or on the wrists is enough. There's no need to spray it on like deodorant. That will just be offensive to those around you. You may not even be aware that all of you seem to have lost your sense of smell, so if you think you can detect the stink of the dog, then your nose must be stronger than even that dog's nose!"

She had hit the bull's-eye, because they all instantly blushed. There was no refuting what the young woman said.

"In fact, the pup's shampoo smells quite nice."

She smiled at Ami, who nodded happily in agreement.

"Ken's shampoo smells like flowers!"

Very nice, indeed. The young woman turned back toward the housewives. Her expression was serious again.

"Humans have an advantage over dogs. No matter how much noise they make, no one's ever going to put them in a cage."

This young woman seemed to have hijacked the argument away from Tokié, who was trying to think of a way to undo the situation when the young woman's boyfriend added his own punch line, with spot-on delivery:

"And you can't buy good manners from a ticket machine, can you?"

Just then the announcement came over the speaker, "NEXT STOP, TAKARAZUKA-MINAMIGUCHI. TAKARAZUKA-MINAMIGUCHI."

The queenpin of the housewives suddenly stood up.

"Ladies, let's get off here."

"Uh, but aren't we supposed to be going to Takarazuka . . . ?"

"Thanks to all these people, I don't feel like it anymore. Let's have our lunch today at the Takarazuka Hotel."

As the train slowed, the housewives hurriedly prepared to disembark, and once the train stopped and the doors opened, they all filed out.

An absurdly heavy scent of perfume lingered after them.

The queenpin had name-dropped the jewel of a hotel along the Imazu Line, which also seemed to linger.

"Wow . . . having to deal with all of them could spell disaster for the hotel!" the young man said.

"Maybe I was a bit harsh." The young woman's expression was contrite.

Tokié broke into their conversation.

"Don't worry—that hotel has history and prestige on its side. They'll know exactly how to handle them."

"I certainly hope so," the young woman said pleasantly, making no move to sit in any of the still-vacant seats, instead heading toward the far door in an attempt to escape the intense lingering odor.

"I must express my appreciation. Thank you for coming to our aid."

"Not at all, it wasn't . . ." The young woman looked down, sheepishly.

Her boyfriend nudged her. "You can be surprisingly feisty." He laughed. "Without always thinking about the consequences, which can be a worry sometimes!"

*And you there, you've got quite the sharp edge yourself*, Tokié thought.

"Yes, but today I figured it was justified to jump in," the young woman said.

*Seems like she's got the reins firmly in hand*, Tokié thought.

"Well, I'm grateful to you for jumping in."

"I was afraid you'd think I was meddling."

Her boyfriend laughed puckishly.

"I'm sure you have the assault capacity to have defeated them on your own, but it's better that you had reinforcements from the granddaughter and her pup to lay siege to those old ladies."

"That's right—thanks to you, it was over in a flash."

"It's true, winning is about believing you can win," said the young man with another amused smile.

The young woman stooped down to meet Ami's gaze, and then she peeked into the carrier.

"So cute, is that a miniature dachshund? Is he your dog?"

Ami was about to nod happily in response to the young woman's question—whereupon Tokié chimed in.

"No. This dog belongs to my husband and me."

Ami pouted melodramatically. "I take care of him too . . ."

"Yes, dear, you do help, but that's all. The dog is mine and Gramps's."

"But Gramps is in the cemetery . . ."

"Ken still belongs to Gramps and me. Like I always tell you." When it came to this matter, Tokié never budged an inch.

"If you want to have a dog of your own, first you must demonstrate the ability to be responsible for taking care of the dog by yourself."

"But I love Ken."

The couple that had given them ground support watched, wide-eyed, as Tokié and Ami did battle. Perhaps they thought that the relationship between the two of them was rather more idiosyncratic than a typical grandmother and granddaughter.

Tokié was aware that everyone seemed to think that grandchildren ought to be doted upon constantly. When she had tea with friends in her neighborhood, they were all amazed by the way she treated Ami, always telling her that she ought not to take for granted how often Ami came over to spend time with her.

"No, dear. Ken is Gramps's and my dog, and that's final."

*Ken, the Kai Ken, is the one who bit my husband on the backside and made him fearful of dogs. That's why I got a smaller dog this time, so that he wouldn't be afraid of this Ken.*

"You're being mean, Granny! You're a meanie!"

"If I'm mean, then all well and good. But you'd better stop making a fuss on the train. If you throw a tantrum, we won't go to the dog run. We won't get any ice cream on Hana Road either."

Hana Road was a promenade that ran between Takarazuka Station and the Takarazuka theater, and it was landscaped with seasonal flowers. Beside the promenade, there was a mall with genteel shops and boutiques, among which was a candy shop that sold Ami's favorite soft-serve ice cream.

"Meanie . . ." Ami may have been unhappy about the situation, but she spoke more softly now.

The young man burst out laughing.

"Gran, you're merciless to your granddaughter! And here was I, thinking grannies were supposed to spoil their grandchildren."

"You may find that I deviate somewhat from conventional standards."

Tokié's response seemed to send the young man into another fit of laughter. At which point the young woman tugged on his sleeve.

"Masashi-kun . . . sorry, but I don't feel well."

At some point the young woman's face had gone pale.

"Ah, it must be the perfume making you sick. Should we move to another car?"

The young man put his arm around the young woman, but then he turned back to Tokié.

"Excuse us—she gets motion sickness. And those women's perfume was awfully strong. We're going to move to the next car."

The housewives' perfume still wafted, if only faintly, around the seats they had vacated, but it did seem to have made the young woman ill.

"No need to apologize. Thank you again for your support despite your queasiness."

The young woman raised her pale face. "No. To put it bluntly, I found those people terribly rude. But I was the meanie. What was I thinking, telling them they didn't know how to apply perfume? I think I wanted to humiliate them."

"You've got guts," Tokié said. She decided against telling the young woman that she reminded Tokié of herself at that age.

"Bye, then."

The young man gave a slight bow and kept his arm around the young woman as they walked toward the rear of the carriage.

*The young man's name was Masashi-kun.*

*It's a pity that I didn't ask the young woman her name.*

## Takarazuka-Minamiguchi Station

Masashi said goodbye to the rather unusual granny and her granddaughter and moved toward the nearby connecting door that led to the rear car of the train.

"Are you all right, Yuki? Do you want to get off at Takarazuka and rest a bit?"

She shook her head as he helped her along.

"No, now that the stink of perfume is gone, I'm fine."

"Do you want to sit?"

There were seats available here and there, although not two vacant seats next to each other.

"I'm fine, it's just one more station. I can stand with you."

They had an unspoken rule for when the train passed over the iron bridge that spans the Mukogawa River—it didn't matter whether they stood by a door or not, but they always faced the side of the train that looked out over the river.

The vast sandbank that was visible from there had gone back to being just a sandbank.

The first time they had ever talked to each other, there had been a giant kanji character assembled in stonework on that sandbank.

At the time, Masashi didn't expect anything to come of their conversation on the train about the kanji character Yuki had spotted on the sandbank—the one that made her thirsty for a draft beer in a glass mug—and that most people paid no attention to. Masashi had seen Yuki, whose name he didn't yet know, as a rival and assumed that she hadn't noticed him. She was constantly snatching interesting books from under his nose at the library. Much to his chagrin, because she was definitely his type.

That day, as she was getting off the train at Sakasegawa Station, she had said to him:

*The next time we meet, we should have a drink.*

*The central library. You go there a lot, don't you? So then, next time we meet.*

So it turned out that he wasn't the only one to have noticed. She had locked on to him as well. And from the moment he became aware of this, he was a goner.

He leaped off the train to rush after her and to invite her, breathlessly, to go for a drink now rather than later. Luckily she was free and happily took him up on the offer. They had also exchanged phone numbers—this all progressed so easily that it made him doubt his own luck.

The start of their relationship was perhaps even more mannerly than a couple of high school kids. On the Saturdays when they could both go to the library, they would meet up at Sakasegawa Station. One way they differed from high school students, though, is that sometimes on their way back they would have a meal together that included alcohol.

Whenever they went to the library, the two of them always gazed down at the sandbank.

生

*It's still there.*
*Yeah, there it is.*

It appeared that someone was maintaining the kanji character: in summer, the grasses that would have overtaken it on the sandbank were weeded; sometimes if the stones had eroded and its outline had started to blur, it would be reassembled and fixed back up. It remained there, inconspicuously, for quite a long time.

But after a typhoon and continuous rainy spells, the torrents caused the river to rise and cover the kanji character, so that now it again looked like any nondescript sandbank.

*It's gone now.*
*Yeah, totally gone.*
*It sure held on, didn't it?*
*It lasted as long as it could.*

It might have been around the time of this exchange that they had started spending time at each other's apartments.

∽

Library dates, sometimes followed by a meal.

It was only because of these occasional meals together that he came to realize that she enjoyed her drink. Not a huge surprise, since in their initial exchange she had talked about associating the kanji character on the sandbank with the word "*nama*" and then craving a draft beer. And once Masashi had mustered up the courage to invite her out, the place where they ended up going was her favorite izakaya. The fact that a young woman had a local bar where she felt comfortable drinking alone was proof that she was a pretty serious drinker.

Masashi was no lightweight, but he did fear that he might lose if they ever played a genuine drinking game.

What's more, it turned out she was the type who seemed to show no effects from alcohol. No matter how much she had to drink, on their way home she'd be straight as an arrow. There were never any unguarded moments—so their mannerly dates always stayed mannerly.

What finally crumbled her ironclad defenses was the summer gifting season.

The office where Masashi worked had a tradition: they would set aside all the nonperishable gifts that were delivered to the company in the lead-up to the holiday, and when the day of ochugen—July 15—came around, there would be a lottery among all the employees to give away the goods. It was a decent-sized company that received quite a lot of gifts, which meant there were favorable odds of winning something.

Then, say, if a teetotaler won a case of beer, or conversely a drinker won fruit juice or higashi confectionery, the employees were free to do a "prize exchange" after the drawing.

This year, as chance would have it, Masashi won the prize most coveted by the drinking connoisseurs in the office. It was a magnum of sake from the famed Keigetsu brewery in Tosa, on the island of Shikoku. This was from a well-known client who each year sent fine sake from various regions of Japan.

Any other year, Masashi would likely have been glad to entertain offers for an exchange. He didn't know much about sake, nor did he have much occasion to drink, it since he lived alone—he preferred beer, which he could drink without ceremony.

But this year, he had to fend off his superiors and his boss, who tried to persuade him to trade it. They were sure he wouldn't be able to finish it himself, but he convinced them that he wanted to develop a taste for sake and that it wouldn't go to waste. In the end, he managed to bring home the sought-after prize.

The truth was he had no particular affinity for Japanese sake, not even this celebrated variety, and he rarely drank alone.

But he did like to drink in good company—and now he had a girlfriend who very much enjoyed drinking sake.

When Yuki drank good sake, it seemed to put her in especially high spirits.

She had been the one to suggest from the start that they split the bill on their dates—the exceptions being when they were celebrating each other's birthdays—and she always made sure to check with Masashi before ordering a glass of expensive sake.

And whenever she did, she seemed to truly savor it. Her expression would be so delighted that Masashi always suggested she have another glass, but Yuki always refused. Apparently, when it came to fine sake, her self-imposed rule was just one glass. This ensured that she would appreciate it to the fullest—and also perhaps kept her in moderation.

He imagined that at drinking parties with work colleagues, when they encouraged her to let loose, she probably deflected in a similar way, saying that she wanted to be able to enjoy the taste of whatever they were drinking.

Knowing her appreciation, Masashi was excited to share this rare local sake with Yuki, and he hoped that her curiosity about this renowned brand might serve as a chink in her armor.

He called her on the phone to extend the invitation. It was not the kind of bottle that they could bring to a restaurant or bar. They'd have to drink it at one of their apartments.

"I managed to come into a bottle of Keigetsu sake from the brewery in Kochi . . ."

"When you say 'Keigetsu,' do you mean *the* Keigetsu?!" Yuki had taken the bait. It was remarkable that she knew it by name, considering that it wasn't one of the major sake brands in Japan. "A while ago, I tried it at a bar somewhere in Osaka . . . it was delicious." Her voice was resonant—it sounded as though she was relishing the memory of its taste. "Someone at the drinking party was from Kochi, and he recommended it. He also mentioned how rare it was to come across it around here."

It was true—the sake from Kochi that Masashi had seen in local bars was usually either Tosatsuru or Suigei, brands that were available throughout the country.

"And he told me something else that was interesting. He said that to produce good sake basically requires good water and good rice. Makes sense, huh? Most places that are famous for sake are also famous for their rice, right? Like Niigata. But Kochi is in the countryside so they must have fresh, clean water, even if they're not really known for their rice."

Also true—he had never heard anything special about the rice in Kochi.

"So you'd think they're already at a disadvantage when it comes to making sake, but they regularly win the gold prize at the annual sake awards—like fifteen or sixteen times in a row. I think altogether they've won, like, more than thirty times, so they're way ahead of the rest of the country. I wonder how they do so well when they start out a step behind?"

"Huh, dunno. Maybe they have an exceptional technique for making it?"

"Nope. According to that guy, it's because people from Kochi prefecture are able to overcome their greediness when it comes to sake!"

She was right about that too—it was a well-known stereotype that people from Kochi were drinking aficionados. Even the women. They might say, "Only a sip," and before you know it, they will have downed three liters of the stuff.

That was quite a track record for Kochi, regardless of whether or not they'd had to overcome their fondness for drinking, and it was an amusing story to boot.

But Masashi found that he couldn't just laugh along with Yuki. Despite her genuine mirth as she relayed the story, he felt a petty, niggling twinge.

He knew that, at their age, of course they each came with a past, though he couldn't help but wonder whether this person that Yuki talked about had been someone special to her, and Masashi would find it troubling if he was still in her orbit.

"This guy from Kochi . . . is he senior to you at your company?"

"Yeah. We still work together."

Did the fact that she could speak about this person so serenely mean that, if they had been boyfriend and girlfriend, things had ended amicably? And if so, that they were still in such close proximity could mean there was a not-insignificant chance of them getting back together.

"This guy fits the three-liter stereotype too," Yuki added.

"You might have said so before," he blurted out.

"Does that worry you?" Her question murmured into his ear over the phone.

"I hate to admit it . . ."

"Sorry. Well, that's reassuring." But Yuki kept right on talking before he could ask her what was reassuring. "I guess I could come over to your place to drink it. You're in Obayashi, right?"

The arrangements were made—the date was set for that weekend, the meal would be teppanyaki, using his hot plate—and Yuki said good night and hung up.

On the appointed day, Masashi cleaned his place meticulously and went to the station to meet Yuki at the agreed-upon time.

They bought groceries at the supermarket in front of the station and were on their way to Masashi's apartment when they passed by the library.

"Wait a minute, the west branch of the library is in Obayashi?! Does that mean that you use both this one and the central library . . . ?!"

"Well, yeah."

"That's cheating!"

"You say it's cheating, but it's only one stop away from Sakasegawa. You could come here too."

"But from Sakasegawa I'd have to go in one direction to get

to the western branch here and then in the opposite direction to go to the central library—that doesn't make sense! I wish I'd known, I would have looked for an apartment in Obayashi!"

"I guess so, but Sakasegawa's pretty convenient, right? And then you're closer to the bigger library."

"You do have a point, but . . ."

While they were talking, they reached Masashi's apartment, and he invited her inside.

He found it amusing that the always fearless Yuki seemed a bit reserved as she stepped into his place. Maybe she was nervous; her eyes darted around the room curiously.

"It's pretty neat, isn't it?"

"I cleaned it today. It's usually a bit messier."

It was a studio apartment, with a kitchenette stuffed into the hallway that consisted of an odd little sink and a single electric burner. He hardly ever used it—if friends came over to drink, he pulled out the hot plate or a cartridge stove.

Knowing these were the conditions, that was why Yuki had suggested they could use the hot plate for teppanyaki, so they could grill things to accompany the sake.

"What do you usually do for your meals?"

"I get onigiri from the convenience store or prepared food from the supermarket we went to."

"Wow, I bet you don't get enough vegetables. Tonight you'll have your fill." And she set about cutting up the vegetables in his cramped little kitchen.

They had met up in the late afternoon, so by the time they'd finished their preparations, it was dinnertime.

They started grilling the meat and the vegetables on the hot plate, and at long last, the Keigetsu made its appearance.

Yuki let out a cheer. "Amazing—a magnum! We'll really be able to savor it, won't we?"

Masashi wasn't sure what to make of her statement—did that mean she intended to come back here again? Or that he could bring it over to her place sometime?

As Yuki devoted her attention to the first glass of this extravagant indulgence, her delight was apparent. Masashi, who was tasting Keigetsu for the first time, now understood what all the excitement had been about.

"Shall we have another glass?"

After much hesitation, she finally agreed to a second glass, but when he offered to refill it a third time, she covered her glass with her hand.

"Later I will have one last glass," she said.

They then switched to the beer that they had picked up, and they chatted about silly things while they watched TV. Before long, the clock struck midnight.

They had both been pretending not to notice how late it was getting.

And in the distance, they could hear the signal at the train crossing.

"That's your last train," he said.

"I know," she replied.

"Guess you're staying over."

"If you were gonna send me home now, I'd burst into tears."

Yuki stood up, her glass in hand, and went to the kitchen.

There was the sound of water running as she rinsed her glass, followed by her steady footsteps as she came back into the room.

"I'll have my last glass now. And then, I'd like to take a bath."

Masashi poured her a third glass of Keigetsu, but he declined when she offered to pour his in return.

"Better not. I can't hold my liquor like you."

He switched to mineral water to sober himself up a bit.

As Yuki took tiny sips of her third glass of sake, her voice became querulous. "Now I'm worried. I hate to think that you don't want me to be here with you like this."

"Where did you get that idea all of a sudden?"

"Because you haven't even tried anything!"

"If you want me to, you have to give me a chance. Like even now, you're as steady as a rock, you're so rational that you even think to rinse out your glass before having more sake, and most of the time, we're out together somewhere. It's not like I can put the moves on you and suggest we go to your place or mine. You could make it easier on me too, you know."

"But I wouldn't let you go home tonight," he finished saying, starting to get sulky now.

"Fufu." Yuki giggled as she gulped down what was left in her glass.

"Really? You swig that like it's swill."

"Because I need to take a bath now."

The fact that the bath was more important than savoring the last bit of Keigetsu was perhaps the surest confirmation of her attraction to him.

When the train crossed over the iron bridge, Takarazuka Music School came into view, the refined building looking like it came out of a fairyland, with its outer walls made of beige brick and its bright orange roof.

As the train rounded the curve and entered Takarazuka Station, Yuki staggered and grabbed on to Masashi's arm.

Ever since that night, she no longer hesitated to lean on him.

The train stopped, the doors opened and the passengers emptied out all at once.

Amid the crowd, they could easily pick out the granny with the dog carrier, a dachshund's head sticking out, and her granddaughter, and as Masashi and Yuki waved at them, they saw them and waved back. They were getting off at Takarazuka, like they had said, and were headed for the descending staircase.

Masashi and Yuki were transferring to the train bound for Umeda that was waiting across the platform.

AND THEN

# Takarazuka Station

After the two of them spent their first night together, they had talked about all sorts of things and much came to light.

Masashi thought that Yuki was always snatching up the books he wanted to read, but apparently Yuki's interest was also piqued by the books that Masashi chose.

*Hmm, I wish I could ask him what made him pick up a book like that*, she had mused.

When he learned that she had felt that way, it pained him to recall how he had pegged her as a rival he was always competing against.

—I wanted to find a reason to start talking to you, but I didn't want you to think I was a weird chick.

—I was frustrated to always just miss out on the books I wanted, but your other books—the ones I hadn't been vying for—impressed me too. You seemed to have good taste.

—So, wait, you mean you disliked me?

—Do I really need to say that it was all the more frustrating because you were just my type?

—No, I get it. You were my type too, only I wasn't frustrated.

I thought it was lucky that time when we were both on the train, that it was my chance to say something to you.

—So, after we changed trains and you came and sat next to me, that was on purpose?

—Yeah. I wanted to show you the sandbank.

—Why?

—I figured if you were the kind of person who saw it and started talking about it with me, then you might be someone I could really like.

—So you're saying that you really lured me in, huh? Thanks!

—Why?

—If you hadn't lured me in, I'd never've had the courage to lure you in myself. You would have been disappointed, or even worse, had sour grapes or something.

—But you came running off the train after me.

—Because I was already lured in!

—Well, I'm glad to know that we were both aware of each other from the start, Yuki said, opting for an extremely peaceable conclusion.

∽

The Umeda-bound train was quite empty, perhaps because it was a local, and even though they were only riding it for one stop, Masashi and Yuki took a seat.

While they waited for the train to depart, Masashi had a question.

"Hey. Do you want to know the reason behind the kanji character on the sandbank?"

## The Passengers on the Hankyu Line

Although the kanji character had been washed away and now it just looked like any other sandbank, it was still special to them.

Masashi knew the truth about the stones that had been assembled in the form of a kanji character. He had looked into it after Yuki had pointed it out to him.

Apparently, several years after the Great Hanshin earthquake in 1995, the kanji character had been constructed as an art installation on the sandbank, as a sort of hopeful wish for the region's rebirth. It had gone through a restoration, and that had just happened when the two of them had first seen it together.

"Uh-uh." As she had the first time they met, Yuki rejected the idea of knowing the facts behind it. "As far as I'm concerned, I already found out what its meaning is."

"Its 'meaning'?"

"It's our god of matchmaking." Yuki pressed her hands together briefly when she said this.

After all, her initial association with it had been a draft beer—which was quite off the wall, compared with the meaning that the original artwork had intended—though it made sense that she would first think of it as a prank and later assign goodwill and affection to it, in keeping with her always positive outlook.

*Come on now, give me a break.*

*First she expects me to go along with her inexplicable idea that the sudden appearance of the kanji character on a sandbank is simply clever graffiti, and then to believe that it's our god of matchmaking?*

*And these are exactly the reasons that I'm crazy about her.*

"Yuki, remember when you said that I was cheating because I could go to both the western branch and the central library?"

"Yeah, sure, and I still think you're cheating!"

"In that case . . ." He prayed to the god of matchmaking or the god of the sandbank to come to his aid, as they had for Yuki. "What if we looked for a place together in Obayashi?"

Yuki's eyes widened. "You mean . . . ?"

"Uh-huh, both of us are the right age, aren't we? You're not planning on staying single, and you have your future to think about. As for me, I'm in favor of living together before marriage. Not necessarily in order to determine if the other person is 'the one' or for any particularly ulterior motive. But because everyone grows up in different environments, with different family rules, you know? This way, we can find out whether those differences complement each other."

*Stop looking at me like that, Yuki, you're going to burn a hole in my forehead.* Masashi forced a smile and scratched his head.

"And then if we do complement each other, maybe, you think, we oughta get married?"

Yuki looked down and then she squeezed Masashi's hand tightly.

"Let's hope we can find a good place to live."

Yuki's reply coincided with the announcement for the train's departure, and Masashi squeezed her hand back in response.

*FIN*